SELECT PRAISE FOR
Norman Lock's American Novels Series

"Shimmers with glorious language, fluid rhythms, and complex insights."
—**NPR**

"Our national history and literature are Norman Lock's playground in his dazzling series, The American Novels. . . . [His] supple, elegantly plain-spoken prose captures the generosity of the American spirit in addition to its moral failures, and his passionate engagement with our literary heritage evinces pride in its unique character."
—*Washington Post*

"Lock writes some of the most deceptively beautiful sentences in contemporary fiction. Beneath their clarity are layers of cultural and literary references, profound questions about loyalty, race, the possibility of social progress, and the nature of truth . . . to create something entirely new—an American fable of ideas."
—*Shelf Awareness*

"[A] consistently excellent series. . . . Lock has an impressive ear for the musicality of language, and his characteristic lush prose brings vitality and poetic authenticity to the dialogue."
—*Booklist*

On *The Boy in His Winter*

"[Lock] is one of the most interesting writers out there. This time, he re-imagines Huck Finn's journeys, transporting the iconic character deep into America's past—and future." —***Reader's Digest***

On *American Meteor*

"[Walt Whitman] hovers over [*American Meteor*], just as Mark Twain's spirit pervaded *The Boy in His Winter*. . . . Like all Mr. Lock's books, this is an ambitious work, where ideas crowd together on the page like desperate men on a battlefield." —***Wall Street Journal***

On *The Port-Wine Stain*

"Lock's novel engages not merely with [Edgar Allan Poe and Thomas Dent Mütter] but with decadent fin de siècle art and modernist literature that raised philosophical and moral questions about the metaphysical relations among art, science and human consciousness. The reader is just as spellbound by Lock's story as [his novel's narrator] is by Poe's. . . . Echoes of Wilde's *The Picture of Dorian Gray* and Freud's theory of the uncanny abound in this mesmerizingly twisted, richly layered homage to a pioneer of American Gothic fiction."
—*New York Times Book Review*

On *A Fugitive in Walden Woods*

"*A Fugitive in Walden Woods* manages that special magic of making Thoreau's time in Walden Woods seem fresh and surprising and necessary right now. . . . This is a patient and perceptive novel, a pleasure to read even as it grapples with issues that affect the United States to this day." —**Victor LaValle,** author of *The Ballad of Black Tom* and *The Changeling*

On *The Wreckage of Eden*

"The lively passages of Emily [Dickinson]'s letters are so evocative of her poetry that it becomes easy to see why Robert finds her so captivating. The book also expands and deepens themes of moral hypocrisy around racism and slavery. . . . Lyrically written but unafraid of the ugliness of the time, Lock's thought-provoking series continues to impress." —*Publishers Weekly*

On *Feast Day of the Cannibals*

"Lock does not merely imitate 19th-century prose; he makes it his own, with verbal flourishes worthy of Melville." —*Gay & Lesbian Review*

On *American Follies*

"*Ragtime* in a fever dream. . . . When you mix 19th-century racists, feminists, misogynists, freaks, and a flim-flam man, the spectacle that results might bear resemblance to the contemporary United States." —*Library Journal* (starred review)

On *Tooth of the Covenant*

"Splendid. . . . Lock masters the interplay between nineteenth-century Hawthorne and his fictional surrogate, Isaac, as he travels through Puritan New England. The historical details are immersive and meticulous." —*Foreword Reviews* (starred review)

On *Voices in the Dead House*

"Gripping. . . . The legacy of John Brown looms over both Alcott and Whitman, offering an example of someone who turned his ideals into unambiguous actions. . . . A haunting novel that offers candid portraits of literary legends." —*Kirkus Reviews* (starred review)

The
Ice Harp

The
Ice Harp

Norman Lock

Bellevue Literary Press
New York

First published in the United States in 2023
by Bellevue Literary Press, New York

For information, contact:
Bellevue Literary Press
90 Broad Street
Suite 2100
New York, NY 10004
www.blpress.org

This is a work of fiction. Characters, organizations, events, and places (even those that are actual) are either products of the author's imagination or are used fictitiously.

Library of Congress Cataloging-in-Publication Data
Names: Lock, Norman, author.
Title: The Ice harp / Norman Lock.
Description: First Edition. | New York : Bellevue Literary Press, 2023. | Series: American novels
Identifiers: LCCN 2022028359 | ISBN 9781954276178 (paperback) | ISBN 9781954276185 (epub)
Subjects: LCGFT: Novels.
Classification: LCC PS3562.O218 I24 2023 | DDC 813/.54--dc23/eng/20220624
LC record available at https://lccn.loc.gov/2022028359

Bellevue Literary Press would like to thank all its generous donors—individuals and foundations—for their support.

This project is supported in part by an award from the National Endowment for the Arts.

This publication is made possible by the New York State Council on the Arts with the support of the Office of the Governor and the New York State Legislature.

Book design and composition by Mulberry Tree Press, Inc.

Bellevue Literary Press is committed to ecological stewardship in our book production practices, working to reduce our impact on the natural environment.

♾ This book is printed on acid-free paper.

Manufactured in the United States of America.

First Edition

10 9 8 7 6 5 4 3 2 1

paperback ISBN: 978-1-954276-17-8

ebook ISBN: 978-1-954276-18-5

In Memory of Myrtle Jane Lock
1930–2018

Her memory is much broken,
and she confounds things sadly.

—RALPH WALDO EMERSON,
in a letter to his brother
William, concerning their
eighty-four-year-old mother

*At Walden Pond, I found a new musical
instrument which I call the ice-harp.*

—Ralph Waldo Emerson,
Journal, December 10, 1836

The
Ice Harp

Foreword

"It is a triumph to remember any word."

TIME SEEMS TO HAVE PREPARED a particularly cruel end for the aging Ralph Waldo Emerson, the nation's preeminent natural and moral philosopher, essayist, and poet of the nineteenth century. Not content with filching memories, it robbed him of words, which were his gift and sustenance. Lectures that he gave on platforms as distant from Concord as Oakland, California, (whose fees contributed substantially to his income) became increasingly impossible. He dealt bravely with his forgetfulness. Ellen, elder daughter, housekeeper, nurse, and mainstay of the Emerson family, wrote of his affliction: "Alone with us, he plays with it [his loss of words] and is very witty in his stumbles. Sometimes, having got through a short sentence, tho' evidently jumping in the dark for his words, he laughs and says, 'It is a triumph to remember any word.'" Only in the initial pages of this novel did I try to reproduce Emerson's lethologia, as the pathological condition is known. (To have persevered in it would have been tiresome for both writer and reader and accomplished nothing of substance.) Thereafter, I made sparing use of malapropisms and spoonerisms, as well as borrowings from old songs and nursery rhymes, to suggest the disordered mind that led him to call his dressing gown "the red chandelier" and his umbrella by the witty circumlocution "I can't tell its name, but I can tell its history. Strangers take it away."

I have given Emerson an articulateness that he likely did not possess in his final years. (Memory began to fail him as early as the summer of 1871, ten years before his death.) To have denied him clarity would have made the book pointless. He must speak cogently of his past and of his present dissolution. I offer a sly justification for his lucid state of mind in this exchange:

> *"Your memory seems as muscular as ever, Waldo."*
>
> *"On that little word* seems *reality teeters. But yes, Mr. Whitman, this is one of my good days."*

I ask readers to accept his "remission," as they do Spoon River's talking dead or Emily Webb's unhappy visit to the living after her interment at Grover's Corners cemetery, in Thornton Wilder's wistful play *Our Town*. (*The Ice Harp* can be thought of as a play for voices.)

In *The Ice Harp*, Emerson's conversations with his distant and departed friends should be understood as occurring within a consciousness fretted by doubt and the isolation that illness can sometimes bring. (As far as I know, the actual Ralph Waldo Emerson did not suffer from delusions.) As for the historical commentary that I have interjected into the novel, I considered it necessary to our understanding of the man and his universe, so distant from that of our own in the twenty-first century, already nearly a quarter past. This commentary is equivalent to the ground base of knowledge that lies, like a sounding board, within us and of which we are hardly aware. On it, we act or abstain from acting. (Whether to take up arms or not is, ultimately, the moral question posed by this novel, as it was in the fifth book in The American Novels series, *The Wreckage of Eden*.)

A note on how to read this book: Italicized passages set off by quotation marks represent Emerson's "conversations" with his spectral guests. They are unheard by any actual persons present. His unspoken thoughts, asides, and soliloquys appear with neither quotation marks nor italicization. (At times, Emerson, his ghosts, and the other real characters talk at cross purposes.) Mostly, I have made do without speech tags, considering them inappropriate to a dramatization of Emerson's beleaguered consciousness. The form of this novel is polyphonic and mongrel, containing elements of traditional narrative, poetry, song, history, and closet drama. It is an imperfect biography of its subject, as well as an autobiography of my thoughts and feelings to the extent that I am aware of them.

My mother died of one of dementia's final stages as I was writing an early draft of this novel. That good woman, who read the great books of literature, kept diaries, and liked to salt her letters with literary quotations, suffered the insult of forgetfulness—of words and, at the last, of the use of her tongue, which could no longer perform its essential function. My mother's bewilderment became, for me, Emerson's own. My thoughts concerning her slow dissolution are the sympathetic resonance of this novel. As the Sage of Concord said regretfully and, at the same time, wonderingly, "Strange that the kind heavens should keep us on earth after they have destroyed our connection with things."

Concord, Massachusetts

OCTOBER 21–22, 1879,

Two and a Half Years Before the Death
of Ralph Waldo Emerson

I

Every mind must make its choice between
truth and repose. It cannot have both.

—R. W. Emerson

"WHAT IS THIS CRUMBLESOME THING?"

"Toasted bread, Mr. Emerson. And will you please stop poking at it?"

"Tastes like straw."

"What a mess you're making! And I just put away the broom."

"And Pharaoh said to his overseers, 'Ye shall no more give the people straw to make brick, as heretofore: let them make brooms.'"

"Whatever are you going on about now?"

"What rots, neglected in the rain and ricks."

"Mr. Emerson, eat your breakfast."

"What is this implement?"

"It's a spoon, dear."

Spoon. Lovely in the mouth—word and thing of the word when jammed with mulberry or quince.

"Husband, don't play with your food."

Neither quince nor mulberry nor yet the common apple. It sits lumpishly on my tongue.

"Pease porridge, if I do not mistake."

> Pease porridge hot, pease porridge cold,
> Pease porridge in the pot nine days old;
> Some like it hot, some like it cold,
> Some like it in the pot, nine days old.

I scoop out the heart of the porridge; I agitate it to beat all; I give it a proper dashing!

"How sweet the words used to be! Not that I ever spoke with the fire of Webster, Father Taylor, Clay, or even gasbag Whitman! I should never have sent him my greetings at the start of a great career. I begged him to get rid of the sex in *Leaves of Grass*. Naturally, he wouldn't."

Wife removes a tub of boiling water from the stove and sets it in the sink.

> Ride a cock-horse
> To Banbury Cross,
> To see what Tommy can buy;
> A penny white loaf,
> A penny white cake,
> And a two-penny apple-pie.

"The man's nothing but a gabbing, loafing prick in a slouch hat!"

"Anymore you talk like a hooligan! I won't have it!"

"Will you wash out my mouth with soap, Lidian, old girl? Oh, not the lye, spare me it!"

I strum the airy lyre. I stick out my tongue waggishly.

Syllables may not have tripped lightly on my tongue, but on the lecture platform, I was smoldering. The ladies adored me. They hung on my every word. I held them in my hand. This woman's hands are floury.

"The ladies adored me, Lidian, as I stood beside the philodendron leaves and orated. My words took whinge."

Not *whinge*, surely, Emerson, old fool!

"What fiddle-faddle, Mr. Emerson!"

In the water boiling on the stove, Lidian stirs dirty dishcloths with a thing whose martial-sounding name chimes pleasingly with *faddle* . . . *paddle*. . . . Pshaw, Waldo, you've become a postman chasing fare-thee-wells blown from his bag of wind. I speak of words a-going, if not yet gone—not quite, only out of reach, just, and justing toward silence, which the dear one keeps. How I could joust, once upon a time!

"I was a veritable Lancelot in the lists, my dear."

Imperturbable Walt and his lists interminable! How tiresome he's become!

"Has he come, Queenie?" An endearment that befits her dignity.

"Has who come?"

"The village postman with his leather bag! I'm expecting a poem from old fart Whitman, 'singing the phallus / Singing the song of procreation.'"

"Language, Mr. Emerson!"

"My ineffables are buttoned up."

How the ladies used to flatter me! Had I not been a moral philosopher, I'd have plucked them.

"One of the San Francisco papers said of me that 'I was tall, straight, well-formed, with a head constructed on utility rather than the ornamental principle . . . but 'refreshing to look at.'"

I look outside the steamy window. On the branch of the elm tree in the yard, a bird sits. Your wings are broken, Emerson, old bird, and so is your memory. Something in the kitchen air stings; I give my nose a good snuffle.

"Mistress of the house, my nose is looming."

"All the better for sniffing out hypocrisy. Isn't that what you used to say?"

I bat my nose with a finger; I do battle with my proboscis.

Battledore—that's the thing Queenie stirs the dirty laundry with! And there, professor, is one more word, thought lost forevermore, pulled up from the muck. Muck of ages, cleft for me.

"Mrs. Emerson, it's a Hebrew nose. My pound of flesh."

"You know very well you have the Haskins nose."

I peer down its length till my eyes cross.

"It casts a large shadow." I sniff the heated air. "The lye stings!"

"Will you try to write today?"

What's in a nose? I lay a finger aside my own.

"Smut, likely."

"Tsk, tsk."

I remember how Henry Thoreau would turn his face away, pinch his nostrils, and blow the snot from his snout. Disgusting habit! I rebuked him once; he laughed and said why spoil a linen handkerchief when nature's hem will do just as well. He was no gentleman.

"I say, Henry T. was no gentleman."

"You're too fastidious, Waldo."

Henry walks through the door that Lidian opened to rid the kitchen of steam, which has made my eyes water and my nose run. His hair is tousled, his beard patriarchal.

"Good morning, Henry. Did you sleep well?"

"I would have if the carpenter had left me room to stretch my legs."

Henry stretches one leg, then the other, like Lidian's cat Jeoffry, which "can tread to all measures upon the music."

"You never seemed to know what to do with them; they gangled so!"

"They were made for walking." Giving them a critical

squint, he lets out a woebegone sigh of discontent. *"I admit they were not made for dancing."*

"I did enjoy your mad capering."

"In livelier days, I was said to cut a clownish figure."

He does so now for my amusement.

"You danced as though you'd caught fire."

"Not quite the thing for the parlors of Scituate."

He shows his leg, *tendu*, like the foppish Osric of the Danish court.

"Did you never get over your Miss Sewall?"

"She's safely married."

"Safely for her?"

"For me, *old philosopher. I wear my dirty boots in the house as I please."*

"Sing me your soles."

"Being nothing stingy, I'll sing you an entire scale: Do, re, mi, fa, sol, la—"

"Henry, show me the bottom of your clodhoppers!"

Treating me once again to the boyish smile of his former days, he tucks one leg up behind him for my inspection of the article in question, sets it down, and, with the other, does the same. I think that he resembles a scarlet ibis gawking by the river Nile and congratulate myself on the metaphor.

"Hallelujah! You remembered to use the boot scraper. I'd have been given the fatal asp by the Concord Cleopatra had you muddied her floor."

"Mr. Emerson, what *are* you staring at?"

"The floor, Queenie. It's vermiculate."

I say nothing of the crumbs of toast, lest she turn her broom on me.

"You mean *immaculate*."

"I do indeed. Why, I'm no better than Mrs. . . ."

"Malaprop."

"The same. Remember, Queenie, the night we saw Macready play Captain Jack at the Melodeon?"

Henry takes a straw from his mouth, with which he has been picking his teeth.

"I prefer the 'tongue slippers' of Constable Dogberry. Sheridan can't hold a candle to the divine Will."

"It was at the Boston Theatre, on Washington Street, where we saw *The Rivals,* but Mr. Macready had no part in it. He played the Danish prince in *Hamlet.* I remember his performance vividly, since you sneezed just as he discovered Gertrude at her prayers. The poor man forgot himself and glowered across the footlights to see who could have been so outré as to honk at such a moment."

"Sometimes, Lidian, you make me feel like a schoolboy waiting for the knuckle rapper for having misconstrued his Latin."

Henry cracks his. I fume. Lidian bites her tongue, as the saying goes.

"Mr. Emerson, do you feel able to set down your thoughts this morning?"

Her voice is kind, but my thoughts lie helter-skelter, like bricks spilled from a hod. To think that straw should have been the binding part!

I address myself to my lanky friend: *"I suppose you find the next life dull."*

"I was given a bean field to hoe, although for the life of me, I don't know why, since we neither hunger nor thirst."

"You mustn't grumble. God knows men, and men, even dead ones, need to be occupied."

"Punished, more likely, as I am denied the harvest. My beans ripen and cannot rot on the vine, nor can I pick them—no, not a single blessed one. It's considered a great sin to interfere in perfection."

"So there is sin in heaven, too."

"It exists in potentia, *as it did for Lucifer before his headlong fall over the banister of heaven. How I detest the idea of eternal life!"*

"Eternity is a human idea, and time is what passes in the mind."

"Good Lord, Waldo, didn't my mind have enough of beans, and beans of it? It would rather that I played my flute or took soundings of the ponds."

"Ponds, you say! How nice for you. How's the fishing?"

"Not ideal, because the fish disdain the worm."

"Queenie, I would like a fish for supper."

"What kind of fish?"

She is wiping her soapy hands on her apron.

"Oh, you know, one that swims, or did swim when it was in its native element."

> Memory, hither come,
> And tune your merry notes;
> And, while upon the wind,

Your music floats,
I'll pore upon the stream,
Where sighing lovers dream,
And fish for fancies as they pass
Within the watery glass.

"I think you'd finish your breakfast before worrying about supper!"

Henry fingers the Adam's apple underneath his beard.

"We hook ourselves, as we did in life."

"It may be hell after all—the place, old friend, where you fetched up, though I'd hate to have the priggish Calvinists proved right."

"Maybe so, Waldo, maybe so."

Musing, he chews on his piece of straw.

"Henry, is there much talk of the future where you come from?"

"Having none ourselves, only a few of us take an interest in yours."

He pretends to see the future through a telescope formed by the O's of his encircling fingers. Dirty and ragged, his nails are quite out of keeping with a state of bliss, I think, until I remember that he labors in other fields than those where lilies grow. Evidently, heaven is arranged according to the principles of Marx and Engels.

My voice catching in my throat, I ask him, *"Will it be as you feared?"*

"Humankind's future is a dismal place of sooty train

*sheds and grindstones on which human noses grow for-
ever shorter. I don't recommend it."*

With a clap of his hands, the make-believe telescope folds up and vanishes.

I pull my lower lip pensively before shaking off
the grim forecast.

*"How I miss the days when Bush was noisy with
onions and controversy!"*

*"Strong opinions, like onions, will keep the crowd at
bay. And for that reason, I like them both."*

"Henry, do you see any of the old contrarians?"

"The dead ones, mostly."

I look at my palms, as though I might see the
dear faces imprinted there: that of Bronson Alcott,
Theodore Parker, the Ripleys, brave Margaret Fuller,
whom the world deemed immoral, Jones Very, who
got drunk on the Holy Ghost and spent a month,
insane with God, at the McLean Asylum, writing
a penetrating essay on Hamlet and his problem.
Gloomy, silent, and watchful, Hawthorne would join
us, on occasion, as did Henry, who preferred to listen
to wind and water and birds than to the high-flown
sentiments of men. What a gathering of genius that
was! The Transcendental Club was the granite on
which our soaring thoughts found bedrock, if only
for a time.

"Do you remember the exultation of those days?" I
sigh, a sound expressive of regret in all the languages

of men. "*This morning, in my shaving mirror, I saw a moist, cold element.*"

"*When I see my face reflected in a slab of polished granite, I think of Jeremiah crying for Jerusalem.*"

Henry tosses his head, so that his long hair flies wildly about him.

"*Your hair is spectacular!*"

"*It grows apace in the rarified air of what the slothful call heaven. What's more, it does forever, or so I'm told.*"

"*As long as that! And do a man's brains also grow?*"

"*Mine are still pickling. And for your information, Waldo, the next world is peopled by women, too.*"

"*I pray that God has given them the vote, for men will never do so. Have you any news of Margaret Fuller?*"

Feeling my face flush, I turn my head from Henry's gaze, forgetting that he has acquired a measure of omniscience. He can see through me to my back collar button.

"*You old dog, Emerson; you ancient roué!*"

I color even more, until Henry is moved to relieve me of my embarrassment.

"*She's in the neighborhood, though the self-righteous shun her.*"

"*She got over her drowning, then.*"

"*We all get over the manner of our dying, Waldo. We inhabit the next phase in perfect equanimity.*"

"*That ought to please the randy old cock Whitman. God spare me from an eternity of his barbaric yawping!*"

"Like everything else, his Leaves *will have their season till they, too, fall into obscurity."*

Thinking of the dying leaves and of the Edenic couple, which paradise shed, I sing:

> We long to see Thy churches fall,
> That all the chosen race
> May with one voice, and heart and soul,
> Sing Thy redeeming grace.

Lidian shakes a hostile finger at me. "Thy churches *full*."

"I love the fall. To be abroad in it . . . out and about."

"There's plenty needs doing in the yard, Mr. Emerson. You can start by dismantling the cucumber frame; the wood is rotten."

"I recall the afternoon Henry built it."

"It wasn't me."

"It wasn't I. *Nominative case."*

"Still the same old pedant, Waldo!"

"Grammar is gravity, without which words would become nonsensical, like a clockwork planetarium gone mad."

"It was Samuel Long, the runaway slave, who built the cucumber frame," says Lidian, whose mind is less moth-eaten than my own. "Henry Thoreau was responsible for the Alcotts' preposterous summerhouse."

"'Tumbledown Hall!' I can smell the cedar shavings curling from his plane."

"It embodied, in wood, the universal principle of impermanence."

"Queenie, whatever happened to Samuel?"

"The last I heard, he was in Philadelphia, working for Elijah Weaver's paper."

"I'd forgotten all about him."

"I'm certain he hasn't forgotten you, husband."

The kitchen has turned tropical; the windows drip with steam; I wipe my sweaty brow. My dear, do you imagine yourself in the hell promised by your Calvinist parents during a childhood "when every lightning seemed the beginning of the conflagration and every noise in the street the crack of doom"?

"Samuel owes you his freedom."

"I grant you that I had something to do with his education. Carlyle, Dickens, and even the perpetually straitened Hawthorne also contributed to his tuition. As to his freedom, no man need be indebted to another for what rightfully belongs to him."

Henry provides the needful correction: *"Or her."*

"I advocated for a woman's unquestioned right to her property in 1855, when I fell under the spell of the formidable Susan B. Anthony. And let us not forget—that is, let me not forget—that I became a suffragist at the dawn of the present decade."

"I'll give the cucumber frame to the cleansing

fire, just as the ancient Romans did their old clothes and furniture every five years."

Lidian points the battledore at me and scowls.

"Don't get any ideas into that head of yours, Mr. Emerson!"

"I should be glad of an idea now and again. I'd also like a slice of pie."

Henry pulls on his ear and chuckles.

"Do you still ponder the universe, Henry?"

"I'm more interested in the behavior of pismires."

"*Pismires.* There's another word I thought I'd lost forever. Or did he say 'pygmies'?"

"Who said, Mr. Emerson?"

"Henry Thoreau—"

"The corridors and chambers of the ants are kingdom enough to ponder."

"And after so many years together, I think you could call me Waldo."

"After so many years, I would find it strange."

"I do miss our little Waldo. He died so very young."

"You're likely to see him soon, the way you've been neglecting yourself."

"Being pure of heart, he may not wish to see me. He may ask God to shut the gate on me, for my sins."

"God is 'the individual's own soul carried out to perfection'—or so you said."

"Then, Henry, I shall shut the gate on myself and throw away the key."

Lidian takes off her apron and gives it a good shake, as if to send my sins flying.

"To tell the truth, Mr. Emerson, I don't feel so near to God as I once did."

All is rags and offal, Queenie.

"The fault is with the calomel you dose yourself. God knows, it's killing you by inches."

Henry leans against the sideboard, paring his nails.

"The people of the future speak of God, when they speak of Him at all, in embarrassed whispers."

"No doubt about it: He has been a disappointment."

"He's getting old, Waldo, and as long in the tooth as the Cohoes Mastodon."

"Queenie is getting old. Her cheeks are wizened, and her face is pinched."

"Time has insulted her, as it does all of us."

"She was never strong. When Waldo minor died, I feared she'd follow him. Ah, but by candlelight and moonlight and in the rosy light of dawn, she is still lovely!"

"You are lovely yet, my dear."

"Mr. Emerson, you're an old fool!"

"Just now I was talking to Thoreau about our Wallie, the little Pharisee."

"Henry's been in his grave these seventeen years!"

"That long? He seems much the same as always. His hands still smell of pine sap."

"You're getting more and more fuddled. One of

these fine days you'll be taking your breakfast in the asylum."

I pay her no mind and ask when our little Waldo died.

"In 1842."

"And in what year do we presently find ourselves?"

"Eighteen hundred and seventy-nine."

"As late as that! It's been quite some time since Jesus walked among us."

Lidian pushes a straggle of gray hair beneath her old-fashioned mobcap.

"Henry says John Calvin's mob is as self-righteous in heaven as it is on earth."

"I wish you wouldn't talk to him."

"Who, Calvin?"

"Henry David! I don't want him in the house. His big feet did enough mischief to my carpets while he lived."

"He was a natural man, if a clodhopping one."

"Are you going to eat your porridge?"

"I don't care for it."

Lumps of matter. How I'd love to taste the fragrant Hyblaean honey I ate for breakfast in Syracuse, overlooking the Ionian Sea!

"I want pie for breakfast."

"You can't eat pie every blessed morning!"

"Pray tell me which of the Lord's days is this?"

"Wednesday."

Henry leans across the table, near enough that I

smell sweat, of all things! Well, better a country odor than the grave's.

"*Woden's day.*"

"Henry Thoreau, you're a damned pagan!"

"Mr. Emerson, my patience is wearing thin!"

"*Patience, patience, patience.* I seem to have forgotten the meaning of that word, except as it applies to a game of cards."

"Hand me your bowl and spoon, if you're done eating."

"This spoon has much to say concerning gluttony; this table talks of ten thousand meals, some eaten in conviviality, others in silence. One need only rest the fingertips lightly on it to receive messages from the spirits of our conjugal past."

Lidian takes the spoon from my hand and the bowl of stiff porridge from between my elbows and sets them in the washing-up tub.

"*To think that I have held ten thousand spoons in this kitchen! Bronson Alcott called it 'the omphalos.'*"

"*He meant Concord, Massachusetts, not the Emerson kitchen.*"

"*The floor is oak, the rug woven of brightly colored rags. The walls are butter yellow. The almanac flutters from its nail. The lamp's glass chimney is bleared with soot. The stove was blackened yesterday by my indefatigable daughter Ellen. The windowpanes divide inside from outside.*"

"Don't belabor the obvious. Or would you emulate Whitman?"

"I'm becoming increasingly unacquainted with subtlety. Although today my mind seems uncommonly agile. Henry, you speak as well as you ever did, despite your years in the ground. I envy you your easy manner."

"I was always—What's Walt Whitman's dandified expression?"

"'Nonchalant'?"

"More pretentious."

"'Me imperturbe.'"

"Loafing with his 'camerados' . . ."

"The jackass!"

"Don't be common, Mr. Emerson!"

"Certainly not, my dear. I was thinking of Mr. Whitman."

"Henry, is the Good Gray Poet dead?"

"Housebound in Camden, living in the home of his brother George. I visited him in his room not long ago. I pretended to be a fly too impudent to be shooed. I buzzed in his ear the suggestion that he should look in on you."

"Two titans of the age reduced to invalids sucking their thumbs. Now there *is a spectacle worthy of Barroom!"*

"You mean Barnum. *Phineas T."*

"To have spent my life kneading words, only to have them turn on me—you have no idea of the anguish!"

Memory is the thread on which the beads of a man's life are strung. And a woman's, too.

Lidian takes the corn broom and sweeps the floor.

She pokes underneath my chair with it. She rattles the legs and rungs. She whisks my gaiters savagely.

"Mrs. Emerson, what do you mean by this assault?"

"I mean to drive you into the yard."

"Am I a goose to be driven with a stick?"

"I won't have you sitting here all day, moping!"

"I am not a moper, and the sky threatens."

"It's a beautiful autumn day."

"*Au–tumn.* I can taste the pippins!"

Lidian takes up her broom against me. She scolds, "Out, out—"

Brief caudal.

"Fortunate are those born with a caul on their heads, for they will not die by drowning. I wonder if poor Margaret Fuller was born so."

"I'll ask her."

"Please do, Henry."

"Husband, where is your mind?"

"In the sweet by-and-by with Miss Fuller."

"She doted on you, and you, husband, on her."

"Did I?"

Strange fits of passion have I known.

"You liked her fair hair, perfect teeth, and vivacity."

"I disliked her habit of fluttering her eyelids and speaking in superlatives. As if a thing could be more perfect than perfect, or made rounder than round by the addition of a degree of circumference!"

"Waldo, my friend, you were in love with Miss

Fuller, who drowned as Mrs. Ossili. If she hadn't fled to Europe, Lidian would have stitched a scarlet letter to her delightful bosom. Hawthorne called you her 'Arthur Dimmesdale.'"

"*Stony-face gave every indication of being in love with her, as well. At the time, however, Margaret was besotted by young Sam Ward.*"

"Humbug, Mrs. Emerson!"

"And don't deny your infatuation for Anna Barker!"

Anna! You were my silver apple of the moon, my golden apple of the sun.

"Queenie, I behaved toward her like a perfect Neoplatonist."

Anna Barker, of the violet eyes and luminous character, whose beauty of form and mind took my breath away, was then the object of Sam Ward's affections. And there was that other Anna—Miss Shaw of the golden meshes of hair and astounding figure, who put me in mind of the goddess Diana. Superb creature! Her shadow on the wall was enough to make me wish us both immortal, so that such perfection would never suffer a decline and I could sit forever and admire it.

Furiously, Lidian applies herself to ridding the kitchen windows of steam.

"It seems that I've stumbled into Robert Fulton's workshop."

"And let's not forget the lady poetess Caroline Sturgis, who was so often underfoot!"

As if I could forget her even now! Ah well! Goethe had his Bettina to dandle chastely on his knee, and I had sweet Caroline Sturgis—whose bottom, I hasten to add, never came within an inch of indiscretion!

"Caroline was in love with Ellery Channing, who married Margaret's sister."

How entangled our lives were then!

Unconvinced, Lidian tatters a spider's web to pieces with her towel.

"Damn the woman, she's exterminated a universe!"

"Shhh, Henry!"

"Louisa May Alcott was another of your conquests."

"She was a mere child at the time!"

"How she would gaze at you with her dark eyes! I would catch her standing in the road, peering through your study window, in the hope of glimpsing her idol."

"Poor thing lost all her hair to typhoid fever during the war. Wonderful chestnut hair, as I recall. Luxuriant. Or does one say 'luxurious' of hair? In any case, you're wrong, Lidian; it was Henry Thoreau she adored."

"Me? I had no idea! At the time, I was in love with Lidian."

"Nonsense, Henry! You were only a boy."

"I was thirty-one!"

"Henry had a face only a squirrel could love."

"Pay her no mind; she's in one of her cross-grained moods."

"Do you have one of your headaches, Queenie? Sophia Hawthorne used to be felled by them. Or is it the old dyspepsia that troubles you? If only we could get to the bottom of your malady!"

"Dr. Clarke assured me that there are several organs he hasn't interrogated yet."

"My face may have been disagreeable to some, but what books I wrote, what poetry!"

"Posterity won't care how awkwardly arranged your features were, Henry. Nor how large a nose I had. I'll have it for a while longer. I may sound the last trump with it."

"Stop your sniffling, Waldo—and please use your handkerchief!"

"Thank you, my dear, for doing me the honor of calling me by my Christian name."

"Not the napkin! Use your handkerchief."

She shies a sopping cloth at me. I take it as symbolic of a rolling pin, or else a cleaver.

"Pinch your nostrils and blow the snot onto the floor as a demonstration of your self-reliance."

"An abominable habit, Henry."

"You were much taken with Charles Fourier's ideas concerning marriage."

Henry is fingering a soft spot on one of Lidian's

Roxbury Russets, as though intending to probe the rotten heart of civilization itself.

"You should have been a bachelor, like me."

In the 1840s, we were all mad to remake society—to rid it of the Calvinist disdain for human passions, save that of making a vain show of wealth, which they bless as proof of divine approbation. The Brook Farmers may have been the best of us.

"And now I think of it, you were in love with the dark-eyed heiress Ednah Littlehale."

"More nonsense! Miss Littlehale was in love with Bronson Alcott."

"And Alcott, with her, whose sexual nature—the old fool maintained—was necessary to the propagation of his thought."

He pushes his finger through the apple's skin. I watch as juice oozes out with relief—or so I imagine, having felt, in my youth, the congestion of the loins.

"Oh, do be quiet, Henry! And that apple was meant for a pie!"

"Mr. Emerson, I've had enough of your company this morning. If you don't remove yourself to the backyard at once, I will—"

"Scream, I suppose; it's what people do when words flail them."

"I will not scream. I'll impale you on the toasting fork."

"But I fear to see the leaves, their flames all but extinguished."

Fork in hand, she menaces me.

"I've never known you to be so out of sorts, Queenie."

She brushes crumbs from my waistcoat with the blade of her hand more emphatically than either crumbs or waistcoat deserves. She tugs me upright by my ear, which, thank God, she does not box. She turns me toward the back door and supplies a Newtonian force sufficient to send me tripping over the sill.

"Your hat, Mr. Emerson!"

She reaches for my soft-brimmed hat and claps it on my head, and before I know it, I'm in the yard, underneath the falling sky, while the plants, those that continue toward winter, rise in their classes, orders, and genera all around me.

My wise aunt Mary Moody liked to say, "If you last the winter, you'll live another year." I wonder if the brave oak, in its ancient wisdom, whispers the same to the trembling aspen.

♣

Each autumn, I rake dead leaves into heaps so that they may be burned. I think that one day the Almighty will send His fallen angels to burn me in perpetuity for having abandoned my pulpit and stopped my ears against His calling. This morning I've come to do battle with them, since my own once greeny leaf is sere.

"Anon, anon, I say!"

The old harrier is rapping at the kitchen window, mistaking the mind's work for idleness.

I give the rake a shake in her direction and scratch the tired earth with its tines. And then I stop, my brain chuffing to be away on the shining rails of thought. How much longer before they rust and the old man, his fire out, is shunted onto a weedy siding and forgotten?

Once more my royal consort raps upon the pane, and I must get down to business.

It suits an old dodderer well to have nature bounded by a picket fence. Henry snorts at convenience. But he has a young man's bones, though they be flensed.

"Is that you, Henry, I hear splintering the brittle leaves?"

"It's Samuel Long, come to stop with you awhile."

He is standing before me now, as he did when Bronson Alcott brought him into my study on a summer's evening in 1845. The young negro had emancipated himself from a plantation in the Tidewater by chopping off his hand and staunching the spurting wound with tar intended for a horse's hooves. Bronson, his daughter Louisa May, Lidian, and I were conductors for the Concord station of the Underground Railroad.

"Samuel, I know you by your empty cuff."

He pulls up his coat sleeve to show me the place.

"Does the stump itch?"

"*It was more than thirty years ago I freed myself, though I can still feel the manacle that no ax can remove, since it bites into the brain's tender flesh. Emancipation is not accomplished by the reading of a proclamation.*"

"*And the War of the Rebellion?*"

He shakes down his sleeve.

"*Alas, not even that has proved sufficient.*"

"*Lidian and I were just speaking of you. You aren't deceased, by any chance?*"

"*No, Waldo, I'm still quick, though my mortal part is elsewhere at the moment.*"

When we were together before the war, he would not have been so familiar.

"*That's fine, then. Your old friend Thoreau has been pestering me all morning. Where is your earthly portion now?*"

"*I'm in Mount Pleasant, Mississippi, hiding behind a magnolia tree while a white mob gets ready to lynch Charles Brown, a carpenter who objected when a white man refused to pay for the house Brown had built for him.*"

"*My first wife's father owned a rope factory in Boston.*"

I smile foolishly, but Samuel appears not to have noticed my stumble into gaucherie.

"The Christian Recorder *sent me to write about the White League and the Klan. I take it you never saw a man hanged.*"

"*It's certain I'd remember if I had. My mind may be clabber, but some things one does not forget.*"

Samuel gazes into the far distance and then

speaks in a tone compounded of amazement and sorrow.

"One would not have thought the human neck could stretch so far." Perhaps he sees the carpenter Brown at the end of his rope, the Kentucky hemp creaking as his boots kick at the air a moment before the living man turns to deadweight and is everlastingly still. *"I'm a coward to be hiding behind a tree."*

"What else can you do?"

Samuel looks at his feet.

"Die for him, I suppose."

"Christ would. You're not by chance He?"

"I am a negro."

"I can see that plainly. Still, I don't see why He could not have been born again as a black man."

Samuel smiles into his empty cuff. He turns his back on me, as though he means to return to Mississippi, where his flesh is waiting.

"Waldo, I no longer believe in the soul of man."

Once, I believed that a soul could neither be created nor destroyed, that not even God had that much power.

"What do you believe in, Samuel?"

"The Fifteenth Amendment. I won't be denied my constitutional right to vote, no matter how many crosses are burned or negroes lynched to discourage me."

"William Lloyd Garrison would be proud of you, if he hadn't died in May."

A wind jumps up and brisks the rusty leaves across the yard.

"Do you recall having insulted him and your people by miming 'Daddy' Rice doing a breakdown and shuffle?"

"I refused to be Garrison's 'well-spoken negro,' trained to show my teeth behind a punch bowl."

I hope Garrison doesn't take it into his head to visit me. His opinions are fiery, and I dread being scorched.

"Do you recall making this cucumber frame?"

"For Lidian, yes."

Samuel crosses the grass to inspect the ruin of his handiwork. He could not have picked a better day for his visit. The sun is gently warming the air, as a candle does brandy in a snifter. Others whose noses are not so gifted (or large) snuffle at the odor wafting from the fields and vines. The odor of rot. I breathe it in—I fill my lungs with it. Here, too, our lives are evident.

"'The summer is past, the harvest is ended, and we are not saved.' Jeremiah."

"I remember being happy when I made you understand why I had behaved like a white man's 'coon' in front of Mr. Garrison."

I recall the moment in my study when I realized Garrison and I had tried to turn Samuel into a demonstration of the evils of slavery, instead of treating him as a man of flesh and blood. Oh, I can see the scars on his back even now, and am very much ashamed.

He higgles with a board; it comes away in his hands from the rot beneath; the nails poke through like a harrow. Like a Hindu widow, the frame longs to give itself to the pyre.

"Whitman would not approve of cremation. He wouldn't deprive the natural worm of its meal."

Whitman! Always there is Whitman, ready to leap at my throat, like a catamount!

"His leaping days are behind him."

"Can you read my mind, Samuel?"

"Naturally."

Lidian is bearing down on me, her eyes sparking, as if she means to ignite the autumnal conflagration with them. Out of apple, she looks as decrepit as old Tumbledown Hall. Not *apple,* surely! Cast your net, Emerson, and see what comes up from the roiled depths. *Plumb.* The very one! The words aren't lost, but merely resting until the time comes when I will— What is that fangled word Whitman is so fond of? *Promulge.* What flatulence! In any case, my words are waiting till I should feel impelled to promulge a new philosophy.

"Mr. Emerson, whom are you talking to? It's not Henry David, is it?"

"Were my lips moving?"

"They were indeed!"

"I did not expect to be observed. I was planning

my attack on the cucumber frame. Ideas must always precede action."

I find I have a hoe in my hand. Perhaps Henry was here after all and left me it. He was a clever man with a hoe, was Henry David Thoreau. Another fine rhyme, Waldo! Ha! I recollect the morning Wallie was with me in the potato patch. He called the garden implement a "hoer." How I laughed at the sweet ingenuousness that would call the implement by the name unkind men give to those women who minister to their loneliness! For so, in his innocence, had he pronounced it.

"Give me that!"

Lidian manhandles the hoe from my grasp. She fumes. She advances on the enemy's rampart. Oh, Lord, how the earth doth tremble! I sweep my eyes round the compass and see Samuel skulking behind the grape arbor. *Courage, man!* I call to him, in my mind. The tempest will soon subside into its pot. Queenie may be fierce, but she hasn't wind enough to rampage.

"May I help, dear?"

Glaring as God did at the Sodomites before He smoked them, Lidian chops the offending planks with the hoe, sending flinders every which way.

"An interesting metaphor, don't you think, Samuel? God as beekeeper smoking His hives."

"Apiary."

"Quite so."

Lidian is gasping like a fish out of water. She throws the hoe into the red chokeberries, puts a hand over her heart as if to keep it from jumping out of her chest, and with a final, if not so triumphant, humph, she strides back into the house.

I remember that, when I was nine years old, I, along with some other boys, went across by ferry to Noddle's Island, in Boston Harbor, to help dig earthworks against the British. What a thirst I had that day! And that night, how wearily I tumbled into bed! The War of 1812 is all but forgotten. The present washes away the past as a hose does blood and gore down the drain in a slaughterhouse floor.

Samuel comes out of his covert, working his tongue to dislodge a seed from one of the remaining grapes. I'm entranced to see the seed between his lips before he spits it on the grass. What corporeality! I say to myself.

"You mustn't reproach yourself, Samuel; there's no shame in skedaddling before a formidable opponent with her head full of steam. In spite of its ribbons, Lidian's mobcap is Phrygian in its chilling effect on me."

I spoon the flinders into a barrow and wheel it to the pit, where, last month, I incinerated a wooden horse that, long, long ago, had belonged to Waldo minor. I kindled the fire with several pounds of yellowed manuscripts.

I rake the gold and ruby amulets—for so the dying leaves appear to be—into heaps that the wind

flusters. Samuel nods approvingly at the little pasto-
rale—scrape of rake, scuttle of dry leaves, mournful
tolling of a chickadee. I assemble the litter into piles
and walk among them as satisfied as Mr. Boffin sur-
veying his dust mounds.

*"You'd better set them alight before the wind scatters
them."*

"Sage advice, Mr. Long."

Glancing toward the kitchen, I catch Lidian's
gaze, as though her eyes were barbed. I touch my
lips to still them in case they have been moving.
Should I acknowledge her with a wave of my hand?
Do I dare to throw her a kiss? She would wonder at
the senile old man's effrontery. I had better pretend
I didn't see her. I'll keep my lips clenched. But I find
myself licking them.

*"Pliny recommends goose grease mixed with gall nuts.
Spiderwebs are also a sovereign remedy for chapped lips."*

For the present, I ignore Samuel and his balms.
I unpack the leaves from their piles onto a tarpaulin
and drag it to the pit. Fire will purge us of impurity,
blood cleanse us of sin. "An altar of earth thou shalt
make unto me, and shalt sacrifice thereon thy burnt
offerings, and thy peace offerings, thy sheep, and
thine oxen." I consider Jeoffry, who is daintily sniffing
a piece of filth in a corner of the yard, a remembrance
of the neighbor's tiger cat. But Lidian would miss her
bedfellow were I to broil him. We will do without
blood, Emerson, and the only aroma will be that of

burning poplar leaves. May it be found pleasing in God's nostrils. I strike a match and touch the flaring head to a leaf and watch the brittle bones appear and shrink to ash. The fire leaps into the air, as once it did in Pudding Lane when London Town burned inside its Roman wall.

> Do you know the muffin man?
> The muffin man, the muffin man.
> Do you know the muffin man
> Who lives in Pudding Lane?

I think I see Henry dancing in an exultation of pyromania, but it's only a sooty wraith of twisting smoke. Prey to a childish impulse, I wave my hat and whoop as the fire salamanders in the flames.

The back door flies open, the hinges grouse, and out bursts Lidian. She scythes through the grass toward me. The wanton flames have turned her teeth to rubies. I stare and stare.

"Mr. Emerson, you've set the azalea bushes on fire!"

I look to Samuel for confirmation, but he has gone elsewhere. Back to his magnolia tree, perhaps. God, spare his neck the noose! I turn to the lufting flames and spit in disdain of the fire element, whose opposing quality is water.

"'Water will quench a flaming fire.' Ecclesiasticus."

"You old fool!"

The Emerson bushes are burning, but God is not here.

She chivvies the fire with a fork. She beats the flames flat with a shovel. They retreat to the edge of the bed; they tremble and lie low; they make a show of submission. Lidian drops the shovel. She sinks to the ground, dirties her cheek with sooty fingers, and laments like Niobe for her children. I help her stand. I give her my arm, and we walk, elderly, toward the house. The sly fire awakens from its smolder, and the old frame's tar-soaked timbers roar into malignant rage. I hear the storm in the wood as the timbers blacken and crack open like burnt loaves. I hear the scrolls and codices shrieking in the Royal Library of Alexandria, set ablaze by an ill wind blown from Roman fire ships meant to bottle up the fleet of Pto-lemy, brother of Cleopatra. In my own way, I have annotated the voluminous chronicle of conflagration, the prodigious history of fire, with a single lucifer match.

I dare not tell Lidian that I can hear earthworms emigrating in terror from underneath the azalea bushes toward the fading glory of the hydrangeas planted next to the rain barrel. Should the wind turn spiteful, "Bush"—our house and habitation—may burn a second time.

"I will beat the rain barrel and pray to Jupiter to open the heavens."

I sing the chorus from Handel's *Die Schöpfung*:

"The heavens are telling the glory of God. / The wonder of his work displays the firmament."

"Husband, you've brought me to my wit's end!"

"A desperate place for anyone to fetch up," I reply, hoping to sound a sympathetic chord.

Wanting to cheer her, I call, "Puss, puss" to Jeoffry, who is cleaning himself in the middle of the yard, as unconcerned by the disaster as Nero was by Rome's. The cat regards me, his back leg stuck up obliquely stiff, and then returns to his nether region. Ah, the ingratitude of cats!

The azaleas, which shed their scarlet petals in June, are again radiant. Flowers of fire are lavishing the sky as flames inundate the hedge. I hear tree roots shrieking in the pit, "Where their worm dieth not, and the fire is not quenched. For everyone shall be salted with fire."

The gate flies open at the behest of a titanic force that breaks the upper hinge. Aeolus carrying his bag of winds steps into the yard.

"I was hoping for a god of rain, not the postman."

Henry leans over the fence and sniggers.

His mockery infuriates me. I snarl a recrimination: *"Woods burner!"*

"Waldo, I told you not to call me that!"

"How many acres of Walden Woods did you burn down? How many woodlots ruined?

"An accident!"

"The good people of Concord would like to have burned

you at the stake. And you never, in your life, indemnified them."

I wipe my runny eyes on my sleeve and see the fool postman smacking smoke with his hat. It's difficult to suffer fools gladly when one is himself a fool.

"Do you have any letters for me?" I ask.

Weeping either from smoke or in frustration, Lidian pulls him by the hand. She shrinks into the shape of a supplicant.

"Mr. Tolliver, do something, please, before the house goes up again!"

The village Hermes throws down his bag, which may contain an offer to publish my collected works bound in red morocco. Seizing the singeing tarpaulin, he embraces the fire and smothers it till not an ember remains. Dissatisfied, he hacks the smutched earth with Henry's old hoe, dividing and subdividing each clod, until I begin to think Tolliver has come in advance of the Fitchburg barons, who intend to run their railroad through my backyard garden. The fire bell that has been ringing in my ears stops. The tunneling inchworms fall silent in their mines. Anthropomorphism is not to be despised, since none can know the faculties of the insect mind.

Dabbing her soot-tracked cheeks, Lidian gives her hand to this Marcus Licinius Crassus dispatched by Jupiter to Massachusetts from the time of Augustus, in answer to my thumping on the rain barrel. He takes her hand shyly in his own.

"God bless you, Mr. Tolliver!"

Oh, the humiliation of it all!

"Don't mention it, Mrs. Emerson."

Wishing to appear in a favorable light, I ask if he will stay for lunch.

Wiping his face with a large pocket handkerchief that, rigged and bellied with wind, could send a toy boat scudding across Walden Pond, he accepts. Like bride and groom, Lidian and her deliverer walk, stately, toward the kitchen bower.

"Door, you ass! Kitchen door."

"Who said that?" I ask, turning on my heels. The yard is empty of all humans, save me.

I stoop to pick the burrs from my bootlaces. My eyes fix on a clump of cyclamen, their diminutive pink flowers previously unnoticed from the grand height of what would be nearly six feet, head to toe, were I not so slumped. How good of the Demiurge to furnish my backyard with loveliness for the otherwise somber winter to come! One needs must give thanks where thanks are due. What if humankind perishes, so long as the cyclamen bloom underneath the ash or snow? The earth abides; her beauties are forever. If we outrage her, she'll sweep us over the doorsill as easily as Lidian does crumbs from the kitchen floor.

This morning as I sat over my porridge, I watched a thin column of ants march, like an army crossing a frontier, from beneath the kitchen door to claim a crust of bread. I marveled at the communal

intelligence and will of the tiny tribe. Of more interest to natural philosophers is the rogue that left the
single file to wander off, alone and careless of such
perils as my boot soles, Lidian's broom, or the merry
cruelties of our local deity, Jeoffry. Here, I said to
myself, is an example of the individual you have
praised—a member of the species *Thoreauvian,* step-
ping to the music of a different drummer. Alone and
apart, the nonconforming beings of our world are
united in their oddity.

The tribal ants carried away crumbs till the crust
was gone and, with it, the necessity that had obliged
them to trespass on the Emerson precincts. Mean-
while, the disobedient fellow—the individualist—
walked its solitary path toward the Hyblaean honey,
which it may never find. If one can imagine befuddlement in insects, that lonely pilgrim was befuddled.
You will surely starve, I said, before you ever set foot
in Canaan Land.

I am left to wonder whether the impulse that led
a few ants to choose freedom was in defiance of the
horde in favor of self-knowledge or a derangement
in the organism that must end in self-destruction. In
other words, were the libertarians of the tribe sick in
body and disturbed in mind, or did they hanker for
enlightenment? Did they, in their extremity, envy the
slaves and wish to be one of them? Or is it enough
for an ant to die on the way to self-fulfillment? Had
I eyes as sharp as a microscope's lens, would I see

the recusants walking as bravely as the three hundred Spartans did to the "hot gates" of Thermopylae?

Speculation will drive you mad, Emerson! There *is* madness among us. You need look no further than brothers Bulkeley and Edward, who would have outshone you had he lived. Strange that two brothers, one backward, almost feebleminded, the other exceptional in intellect and the moral sentiment, should go mad and be confined, as was the case for both of them. I feared that I, too, would be taken, in time, to the McLean Asylum. Lately, I've begun to wonder if I shan't make my last bed there. I'm more likely to die of consumption, which carried off my first wife, Ellen; my grandfather William; Edward; our youngest brother, Charles; Henry T.; and—from what I've read—smothers a third of Bostonians each year. Wasting kings and commoners, politicians and poets, alike, consumption is democratic, though unrhapsodized by the so-called Poet of Democracy.

A boy of the sort my aunt Mary Moody Emerson would call a "ragamuffin," were she still in life, peers at me over the fence. In memory, I can hear her voice—the sharp edge of it that "could cut the head off a tenpenny nail"—admonish the child thus: "If you give me sauce, boy, I'll box your ear!"

Saucebox. What a delightful expression, though, for the life of me, I can't envision the object for which it's named; for all I know, it's sitting in the cupboard next to the gravy boat.

> The Owl and the Pussy-cat went to sea
> In a beautiful gravy boat.

"Are you the admiral of the gravy boat, good sir?"

The good sir treats me to a look for which boys are universally condemned—a mixture of hauteur, disdain, self-confidence, amusement, and a soupçon of pity. Only then does he deign to give me his answer.

"Admiral *yourself*!"

"Is that sauce I hear?"

"Applesauce!"

"Ah! So you've come to steal my pippins, you pleasant rogue!"

He turns his head to regard my apple tree.

"I stole the last good one a week ago."

"I shall box your ear, you rascal!"

The rascal sticks out his tongue and waggles it rudely.

"Just wait till I get my stick!"

He warbles a scurrilous stanza, which admirers of bawdy songs and phallic dances might relish:

> Old man Emerson
> Is a great thinker.
> He preaches to the church mouse,
> Sitting in his outhouse!
> What an old stinker
> Is Ralph Waldo Emerson!

I am not offended by this scrap of scatology. I sometimes think that much good would have come from the pagan settlement at Merry Mount had Captain Miles Standish not chopped down the maypole and scattered the inhabitants.

"What's your name, boy?"

At this moment, he reminds me of Jeoffry cornered by the neighbor's dog; he doesn't know whether to flee or show his claws.

In spite of myself, I feel my good humor leak onto my face and puddle in a smile.

The boy studies my eyes for signs of a grown man's treachery.

"Well?"

Either he has judged me to be harmless or has taken courage in the fence baring its sharp pickets between us. For whatever reason, he decides to indulge me with a choice morsel of his regard. In other words, he is prepared to concede my existence and acknowledge it.

"Billy Spicer."

He gives me his name—not gives, for he is too fierce in pride and self-possession to give me so much. He *lends* it to me, so that I may try it out in my mouth.

"By any chance, are you a poet, Mr. Spicer?"

Without meaning to, I let an old schoolmaster's envy for a vigorous young pupil color my voice with sarcasm. The effect is immediate.

Billy humps his back like a defiant cat.

"I sincerely beg your pardon, Billy. Please help yourself to my pippins."

"There's none to get, Mr. Emerson." You senile old ninny!

I can scarcely recall the days before I was graduated by Harvard, when I enjoyed pulling pranks and other forms of silliness. And here, six decades later, I find myself in the role of Tom Sawyer bandying persiflage with Huckleberry Finn.

Persiflage. It sounds like the name of a villain in a melodrama, or else a parlor snake.

"Billy, you're correct. The pippins are wintering in my cellar. At this moment, however, my good wife has a pudding in the oven, which is, I promise you, an uncommon comestible on the order of manna. Not even a golden apple of the sun is sweeter than one of Lidian's apple puddings."

I let my distinguished nose snuffle in approbation, since a fragrance, such as is borne upon the wind from the Spice Islands to the lucky Dutch plying the Sea of Java, is, indeed, visible in the yard.

Visible. The word seems out of order. Ah, well, let it stand, old man.

"Do you know your Bible, Billy?"

"No."

"Quite right. Make your own bible. Select and collect all the words and sentences that, in all your readings, have been to you like the blast of a trumpet."

His eyes brighten. Doubtless, he is picturing himself regaling the town gossips, who are hungry for examples of the deranged mind of the Concord crackpot. Who am I to refuse to satisfy their hunger?

"Did you enjoy the fire, Billy? I know young boys are partial to fires."

He has his claws out.

"I didn't set it!"

"No, no, the arson was mine. In—we are in the month of October, are we not?"

He humors me with a roguish nod.

"In October of 1871, I walked amid the ruins left by the Chicago Fire. What passed here this morning is small potatoes in comparison."

Unwilling to dwell on ruins or potatoes, I shoo the memory, as if it were a fly.

Sniggering Billy says, "Mr. Emerson, we're in 1879."

A precocious lad, though much grimed.

"Do you play the trumpet, Billy?"

"No, but I can play the jaw harp."

"Better the jaw harp than a lyre. It behooves a man always to be honest."

He gives me a scalding look, a specialty of boys who steal their neighbors' apples.

"And what is your opinion of ants, Master Spicer? Lately, they've been much on my mind. Are those that leave the herd behind them destined for the lyceum or the asylum?"

"My mother pours kerosene down their holes and burns them out."

"The day shall come, even unto pismires, when 'the elements shall melt with fervent heat, the earth also and the works that are therein shall be burned up.' Second Peter."

"Ants get into things."

"That does seem to be the purpose of their corporation. Shall we go into the kitchen and gorge ourselves? Afterward, you can jaw a threnody for the immolated ants."

At this moment, Lidian chooses to show herself, although not as Aphrodite did to Paris. Unlike the naked goddess at her bath, Queenie is dressed demurely in a plain brown bodice and skirt topping Congress gaiters. Her bustle, of course, is modest.

Lately, I seem to be thinking of apples. The golden one that Paris awarded Aphrodite for her beauty, which outshone Athena's and Hera's, had been picked by the goddess of strife from the Garden of the Hesperides to sow discord on Mount Olympus. The other famous apple (for so I believe the forbidden fruit to have been), I mean the one the serpent gave to Eve, had ordinary pips rather than gold nuggets, although the Garden is said to have been glorious.

"Mr. Emerson, are you coming?"

"Coming, Queenie. I've invited my young friend to lunch."

She squints at the boy in disapproval.

"Mrs. Emerson, please be acquainted with William

Spicer, admiral of the gravy boat and a future poet, if I'm not mistaken."

Billy waits with evident apprehension to hear his doom pronounced.

"He's not welcome here!"

The boy turns to me as a man standing at the bar would to his lawyer after being charged with matricide.

"Lidian, if you're thinking of the pilferage of our pippins, I've forgiven him. Or would you have all boys be like Tantalus, for whom the fruit of the tree was forever out of reach?"

"He's done far worse than steal fruit!"

"Hast thou murdered thy mother, then?"

"I never did!"

"What new lunacy is this, Mr. Emerson?"

The boy leaps to his own defense.

"My mother's in Chelmsford, staying at her sister's."

Lidian *pishes* him curtly.

"Last week I caught him stealing a mince pie from the kitchen!"

"Mince, you say? My favorite breakfast pie. Well, Master Spicer, I see you're already familiar with the wealth of the Emerson larder and pantry."

Lidian menaces the boy with a stick.

"Now scat!"

"You had better beat hard for the Indies, Admiral."

"And don't come back!"

"Had it been any other pie than mince, I'd have pardoned you. As Quetelet, the social physicist, has it, 'Society seeds itself with crimes, and the criminal harvests according to his famished condition within it.'"

The criminal element before me sticks out his tongue and scats, tossing over his shoulder a parting insult:

> Old man Emerson's
> The Sage of Concord.
> He lectures the chickens
> On Transcendentalism!
> What an old crackbrain
> Is Ralph Waldo Emerson!

I sigh and go inside the house to hear news of the wider world from the postman, whose mouth seems to possess a superfluity of teeth.

※

"What news of the town, Mr. Tolliver? Has it been taken over by its rats?"

I turned one of Melville's cynical assertions into a question, as befits an invalided mind whose once hard-and-fast convictions have softened into the pabulum of opinion.

"We have no rodent problem in Concord, Mr.

Emerson, excepting the squirrels that got into Mrs. Tish's attic and died there."

"Even the corpse has its own beauty."

Postman Tolliver butters his fingers. Scowling at me, Lidian hands him a napkin—too late, I'm pleased to announce, since he has employed the oilcloth to rid his digits of grease.

"Well, the fellow's no better than he should be."

Whether the invidious remark was mine or Henry's is unclear, though a circumspect peek beneath the table does not reveal the presence of my trenchant friend. I give Henry the benefit of the doubt and shoulder the blame. "I beg your pardon, Mr. Tolliver, if I have given offense."

"None taken." He beavers through his buttered bread.

I stare in fascination at his teeth.

"You've been missed in the town, Mr. Emerson."

"I can walk to the town, but my lucidity, you understand, will sometimes remain behind. The supreme injury, Mr. Tolliver, is that which old age does the mind. Bush is nearer to Sleepy Hollow Cemetery than it is to the town, and I'm assured of a warm welcome when the jet-creped hearse arrives there."

"Well stated, Waldo, old friend."

Henry has appeared. He is polishing an apple on his sleeve. It's as perfect a specimen of *Malus pumila* as any picked in paradise or stored in Plato's cave.

"Thank you, Henry. I had a feeling you were lurking in the vicinity."

"I've been enjoying your antic disposition. You do madness like one born to it."

"I'm not mad, except as words make me so. I'm terrified of their desertion. They fall out of my mind like cogs from a machine."

"You must play the part that's left you. Why not have fun as you go about your dying?"

"I'll try, though I'm an indifferent player."

"Did you say something, husband?"

"I asked Mr. Tolliver if he has any choice tittle to impart."

Who hears more village gossip, grievances, and slanders than its postman? Ours has dismembered the chicken on his plate, disturbed the cranberry sauce, masticated the bread, and drunk the ale I poured him from the stone jug. He takes his time, while I await his pleasure. I don't resent him, because he did me a service this morning. I would never have heard the end of it had Bush caught fire a second time in a decade that promises to be my last as a householder listed in the Concord census before I become a tenant—in perpetuity—of its graveyard.

"Until the land speculators evict you."

"True enough, Henry. If they do not hesitate to put widows and orphans on the street, they won't scruple at mere bones."

"I don't know much in the way of tittle. Mr.

Jarvis at the bank was let go because of 'irregularities.' Clayton Smith got arrested after breaking the arm of Meehan the butcher for giving short weight. Tongues have been wagging ever since the Providence Grays beat the Boston Red Caps, to win the National League pennant. Something's rotten there; something stinks."

I rub my hands together like a fly sitting atop a cow flop.

"Why don't we read the letters in your bag?"

Her mouth stuffed with pudding, Lidian cannot rebuke me, though in her eyes, I see that she longs to fry my gizzard in black butter.

"You know I can't do that, Mr. Emerson; it's a federal crime to read other people's mail."

"Imagine the insights to be gleaned, Mr. Tolliver! I'd think it worth a spell in Concord's hoosegow to acquaint yourself with the self-aggrandizing nature of our kind. Thoreau thought it worth a night in jail to protest Polk's war on Mexico."

"That's all right for them who speechify for a living."

"A windy living, Mr. Tolliver. A grinding and grueling one, I assure you."

"The villagers used to think a Transcendentalist was an expert at pulling teeth."

Lidian chortles, splutters, wheezes, turns red and Pentecostal as she chokes on a mouthful of cobbler and consonants.

The postman looks consternated.

"Mr. Tolliver, if you'll kindly clap her back, the little world at number twenty-eight Cambridge Pike will once more be harmonious."

While Lidian gasps and goggles like a winded grampus, he weighs the propriety of such an assault on her person against the possibility of her expiration. Who knows? He may have a letter for her whose delivery, posthumous, would be as a wrench thrown into the works. As it was in ancient Persia, so it is in America: "Couriers are stayed neither by snow nor rain nor heat nor darkness from accomplishing their appointed course with all speed," thus wrote Herodotus in his *Histories*.

"Sooner than later, Mr. Tolliver, if you please."

He gives her a splayed-fingered whack on her back stays.

"Mr. Tolliver, for the second time today, the Emersons are in your debt."

"My pleasure, R. W."

What cheek the fellow has!

"I wonder if there might not be a letter for me in that bag of yours?"

"I know for a fact there is."

"Would it be a crime were I to read it now, or must I wait till it arrives, in due course, in my mailbox?"

"There's nothing in the regulations against letting you have it now."

He rummages among the envelopes and hands

me mine. Escaped from Aeolus's sack, a storm of passion is loosed upon the air, expressed in the manifold tones of a baffled, bereft, and bilious humanity—grief, grumblings, shrieks, curses, effusions of love, and eruptions of enmity that the tepid prose of the companion catalogs and business correspondence cannot muffle.

"Please close your bag, Mr. Tolliver. It seems all of New England is clamoring to be heard."

Eyeing me with mistrust, the postman shuts his bag, and the voices cease.

Lidian, poor woman, begins to hiccup.

"If you'll pardon me, friend, I'll take my letter outside and read it to the jays. When Mrs. Emerson has conquered her spasms, she'll spoon out some of the cold pudding beloved by our parrot. Not the same pudding, of course, for that went the way of Polly, who perished ages ago, but very like it. One should be a freethinker everywhere except the kitchen, where it is advisable to follow the recipe to the letter. To the letter, Mr. Tolliver!"

🌲

A man's sixth age is oftentimes accompanied by regret that he does not shuffle toward his end "full of wise saws and modern instances" but has arrived at a "second childishness and mere oblivion, / Sans teeth, sans eyes, sans taste, sans everything." The careless days when body and intellect were vigorous are like the fading recollection of the sea for the fish that lies on a boat's planked deck, kissing the alien air. So here stands Ralph Waldo Emerson, seventy-six years old, admired for his moral philosophy, which he hopes will survive him into the next century—that is, if the earth does not crack and ooze like an overripe melon.

On the arbor that Henry built, some of Ephraim Bull's Concord grapes linger. If a grape can be improved by a man, may not men and women be also by their Maker? God, the great propagator—surely He could bring out the sweetness of the race if He chose. Why must He always lay waste to His creation? Were I a Hindu, I would revere the elephant god Ganesha, patron of letters and learning, rather than Kali, the destroyer. Shall I partake of the grapes my neighbor created to thrive in New England's cold?

I place one on my tongue like so. Bah! It's bitter! Perhaps bitterness is the essence of everything fated to be crushed. From the summit of old age, I see the bitterness that our kind is given to endure. I must ask Mr. Tolliver how goes it with old man Bull, whose lungs are bad.

I loop the wire arms of my spectacles around my ears. Ah, a letter from John Muir! I can almost smell sap on the writing paper. It's been—what?—eight years, if I'm not mistaken, since we were together amid the sequoia trees and sugar pines of the Mariposa Grove.

Thin, ascetic, his beard cascading from his chin, a

hard man with a gentle soul like bark on a jack pine, Muir steps from behind a tree. He speaks as God would were He a Scotsman.

"Fennel must be crushed to release its perfume."

"Have you crossed the continent, John, just to remind me that the act of crushing can be needful?"

"Do you remember this by Longfellow?

> *"'Above the lower plants it towers,*
> *The fennel, with its yellow flowers,*
> *And in an earlier age than ours*
> *Was gifted with the wondrous powers,*
> *Lost vision to restore.'"*

"I'm afraid no common elixir can restore my *lost vision."*

"You saw clearly in Yosemite."

"'There were giants in the earth in those days.'"

"Aye, indeed there were."

"I can scarcely recall the man I was then."

"You were fine, Waldo! When we rode out from Leidig's in the valley, I worried that the country would be too rough for you."

"I was already an old man—though I rode a mustang up the mountain trails."

Everywhere, an uprising of granite sheered above black oaks into heaven—a gray sea veined with gold and peopled with clouds.

"Twenty-five miles on horseback through the Sierra Nevada. Not an easy trip."

"For a reedy scholar from the East."

"I admired you immensely before we met, and ever after you've been with me in spirit."

"John, I was about to read your letter."

"Take off your glasses; I'll save your eyes the strain."

"It's wonderful to see you again! You look the same as when I first set eyes on you by Yosemite Creek. You were keen as you showed me your drawings and botanical specimens in your 'study' under the sawmill's gable."

"'To the wise, therefore, a fact is true poetry, and the most beautiful of fables. These wonders are brought to our own door.'"

"Did you write that, John?"

"You did, Waldo, in 'Nature.'"

"This morning I set fire to a parcel of nature outside my kitchen door."

I gesture vaguely at the scorched earth, the splayed gate. A pall seems to drape above the yard, greasy and particulate. Doubtless it is the color and texture of my mind, in the aftermath of the morning's minor apocalypse. I recall poor Job, put-upon by God, as he sat among the ashes.

"Nature is also an idea, and an idea can't be destroyed."

"Maybe so, John, but the idea of a lilac has no fragrance."

"I grant you that, Waldo, nor do your passed-over grapes taste sweet."

"You were eavesdropping on me."

"We're of a common mind, you and I."

"You've come at a good time; I seem to have my wits about me for the moment. That is, if I'm not imagining you."

He will not say. Instead, he expatiates on the condition of my grapes.

"It's not the fault of a saturnine deity, but of the bitter rot that spoils the fox grapes."

The bitter rot has crept into my brain. I've been too long on this parcel of earth, where I now stumble graceless and diswitted. But I keep my disheartenment to myself rather than spoil the sweet temper of this most optimistic of men.

"How's San Francisco these days, John?"

"Cold and damp, like a wet dog come in out of the rain."

I visited the city of seven hills in May 1873, along with my Edith, her husband, Will, and Jim Thayer. My old friend John Forbes secured one of George Pullman's cars for us to do our westering in. Crossing the Great Plains, I saw only a single, pitiful buffalo—the army, railroads, and sporting men from the East having reduced them from their millions to a hundred, more or less. Bleached bones heaped high as a two-story house glared reproachfully in the sun, waiting to become fertilizer, buttons, and stays. At Laramie depot, Indian squaws were begging for pennies, while young bucks lounged in idleness against a blaring wall.

At Ogden, Utah, we went south and stopped at Salt Lake City. I wanted to meet Brigham Young. In spite of his polygamy, I esteemed him for having taught us how to subdue the desert and turn it into a habitable garden. The Mormon fields were fat, their peach and cherry orchards in righteous bloom. Young claimed never to have heard of me. Perhaps fame is irrelevant in a world peopled by saints and incorporated spirits.

In San Francisco, we stayed at the Occidental and dined at Cliff House, dashed by the chiding sea. On the rocks below us, a herd of seals scolded, while we ate beefsteaks and oysters and drank to the health of the great nation we had crossed. At night, our cigars lighting the way, we walked the streets of Chinatown, where men, their hair done in long braids, argued points of view alien to our own, which may be less wise, being less ancient, than we care to admit. They had scrabbled, by pickax, shovel, and dynamite, over the granite roofs of the Sierra Nevada to Ogden, where, ten years ago, at Promontory Summit, their iron rails met the Union Pacific's, begun at Omaha, and the golden spike was driven home. The coolies were excluded from the commemorative photograph.

"California is America's bedraggled hem. Speculators in everything, except philosophy, are there. So are swindlers, peddlers, pettifoggers, sharps, shams, confidence tricksters, and evangelists—former easterners, mostly,

who got drunk on their own ideas of freedom, a limitless one that—"

"Waldo, isn't your idea of freedom also limitless?"

"No, yes—no!"

"In your journal, you wrote, 'I shed all influences.'"

"Hell, John, I don't know what to think anymore! Words are forsaking me, and when the last has gone, will I still be a moral philosopher? Will I be even as much as a moral man, or, for that matter, a man? I won't be a poet—that much is certain, since a poet is a namer of things."

"A jack pine is still a jack pine, though there be no poets to call it so."

"I'm lost in the thickets."

"You've only to follow the setting sun to get clear of outmoded forms and philosophies. 'The star of empire rolls West'—your words, Waldo."

One eats one's words with little appetite.

"Would you have me pick my teeth with crow feathers, John?"

"When you stood on the porch at Cliff House, you muttered to the wind, 'Voices raised in contention, whispered in deceitfulness, or whined in petulance come to an end at the western edge of the continent. Beyond the noise of breakers, the clamor of our kind is silenced. Beyond lies the Orient.'"

"Did it know our hearts, the Orient would tremble."

"It is safe enough, I think, with so vast an ocean between us."

"The black-hulled warship Mississippi *steamed into Edo Bay and fired on the town of Uraga. The shells were blank, but the meaning was clear: The Orient is a pearl, and we must have it."*

A pearl, a pear, someone else's paradise, we must have all and everything, for only that can sate the insatiable.

On the way to San Francisco, I saw the immensity that is America. And yet our appetite for land remains unsatisfied, is likely never to be satisfied. Behold the famous States / Harrying Mexico / With rifle and with knife! Why should we be content with a portion of the continent? Tacked to the wall of McCreary's barbershop is a chromo of John Gast's *American Progress*—an allegory of rapacity, in oil paint, in which a golden-haired and -girdled woman draped in an Attic gown strides through the sky above emigrants westering in prairie schooners and steam trains. Being resourceful, as well as aerial, she strings telegraph wire as she goes, while Indians and bison scatter into the outer dark.

"My great fear, John, is that nature will pass away, just as Cliff House will one day fall into the Pacific—or be conflagrated by some scatterbrained fool. Care for a cigar? I find it a singular comfort."

The cigar was rolled in Havana, a token of the rich prize that is Cuba, waiting, like a ripe apple, to be plucked by the States in the name of Manifest Destiny. I won't tell the Man of the Mountain standing before me that he has taken the island nation between his teeth and bit off its end.

I reach out my hand toward Muir, but I hastily withdraw it before having confirmed the actuality of his presence in the yard.

"You are *here, aren't you, John? You're not a figment of my imagination."*

"Could a figment be smoking a cigar?"

"An inference based on a cigar is weak, in that a cigar contains its own dissolution."

"So does Everest, Waldo, if it comes to that. And so must Cliff House one day succumb to the ocean's wild importunities."

I with my hammer pounding evermore / The rocky coast, smite Andes into dust . . .

"Some mad anarchist's stick of dynamite will do as well."

I reach out my hand again, near enough to his coat sleeve to feel the burr of rough wool. *"I've had several visitations this morning."*

Muir eyes me cannily, like the Scotsman he is.

"Is that so?"

"They left no calling card."

He searches his coat and hands me a cottonwood leaf.

"Mine. Embossed near Yosemite Creek."

I appraise it as Queen Victoria's master of the jewel house would the Koh-i-Noor. The leaf appears the real McCoy, though I am somewhat suspicious of its perfection.

"We are conversing, you and I—are we not? Lidian complains that I talk to myself."

"As long as the talk is interesting, what does it matter?"

I blurt the question that has been fretting me, as the pea did the princess on her mattress.

"Is Henry Thoreau truly dead?"

"The poor fellow died of consumption at forty-four. His writings have meant much to me. Both of you taught me to read in nature's book."

If Henry and I were nature's docents, you, John Muir, have been her principal evangelist. You see what few others do: the belittlement—by little men—of the mountains and the forests. In your calloused hands, you hold a shepherd's crook and the rusted key that Jophiel turned in the lock on Eden's gate and then flung into the wilds after the expulsion.

"Do you recall the purple valise in which I carried my essays to Yosemite? What would the giants in the earth have made of my tiny thoughts had I been bumptious enough to read them aloud?"

"They are of another order of being, Waldo, and their thoughts are God's."

"We drank a purple liquor drawn from sequoia cones you had steeped in water, so that we might apprehend— in your word—'sequoianess.'"

"You don't need an altar rail to receive the blessed cup of nature; a tin pail filled with spruce beer will do fine."

He licks his bearded lips. *"I wish I'd remembered to bring us some."*

Even now I shiver to recall the tumultuous night we easterners cowered inside Muir's hut at the foot of Yosemite Falls while he clung—drenched to the bone and ecstatic—to the top of a giant spruce to feel what a tree feels in a storm. He put me in mind of Odysseus tied to the mast of his ship, so that he might hear the Sirens singing, while his crewmen's ears were packed with paraffin. I stuffed mine with cotton wool. John Muir left the world of men and women to spend his life besotted by wildness. As a young man, he was as clever a tinkerer as Edison and could have been a person of wealth and property had he bothered to patent his inventions. But he does not have an acquisitive soul.

"You're a rich man, John Muir, notwithstanding."

"I'm poor as a church mouse—which is to say, I have all that a mouse or a man requires: crumbs of the Host, wine of the spirit, and a cathedral in the wilderness planted by God. That, Waldo, is wealth and property enough for the most ambitious mouse."

God the planter. Which, I wonder, are we? His tenant farmers or His slaves. I've been like the nonconforming ant, solitary and—who knows?—mistaken in its quest.

Jeoffry comes near to Muir but neither stops nor sidles. Because he takes no notice of my sylvan friend, my skepticism rears once more.

"And you are *here with me, John?"*
"Here, and in the ice mountains by Glacier Bay."

I shudder, but not with cold. I'm a mariner who, all his life, has navigated by the stars, only to find at the end of it that the stars are tumbling from their orbits. Just as gravity holds matter in place, so memory keeps the constructed world from falling into a lump of porridge.

Confusion would be written on my face, because Muir holds out a hand and, with a nod, invites me to touch it, as Jesus did Thomas. I still can't bring myself to do it, afraid I will find it no more substantial than Samuel Long's missing hand. I hear the Sirens trilling. I feel my life slipping through my fingers like raw silk. As we humans often do, I hide behind bravado.

"I'm not like the disciple Thomas, who had need of touching the hole in the Lord's palm to prove His resurrected presence. I'm not a man vexed by doubt."

As though in mockery, the sun slips behind a cloud. Muir trembles like someone standing behind a veil of shimmering heat, and then he disappears. Truly, all things unfix, disport, flee.

> Illusion works impenetrable,
> Weaving webs innumerable,
> Her gay pictures never fail,
> Crowds each on other, veil on veil,
> Charmer who will be believed
> By man who thirsts to be deceived.

Thirsts and *pays* to be gulled, as P. T. Barnum will attest, having made his fortune from the credulous who will, and must, believe in the Feejee Mermaid and Jo-Jo the Dog-Faced Boy.

Unnoticed, Lidian has crept up behind me. She touches my arm. I turn and grit my teeth in advance of her reproaches.

"I'm sorry, Queenie; I've been an ass."

"You have indeed, Mr. Emerson. But I can no more upbraid you for being one than I could if you'd been so imprudent as to allow yourself to be struck by lightning."

The analogy is apt, for I suppose that one whose mind has been galvanized would feel as disorganized as mine does.

"I've tried to will myself completely in the world again."

"It's not for you to will it; only God can."

"He appears to be indifferent to His creation, Lidian."

"He is as you wished Him to be in your youth when you argued for self-reliance."

As men's prayers are a disease of the will, so are their creeds a disease of the intellect.

Muir speaks to me from out of his Alaska: *"God is, and He lives in the wilderness."*

And is happy to be rid of the tribe of foolish Adam and his inquisitive mate!

"I'm no longer young, Queenie. The sky is closing in."

"Then 'Contract thy firmament / To compass of a tent' and be satisfied."

"It's unfair to turn my words against me."

Lidian walks around the backyard like a picket watchful of a foe's approach. Her jaw is set; her lips are compressed. All of her has thinned to gauntness. While I rambled on behalf of humanity's causes, my sick wife had the care of our house and children. She was never right after the scarlet fever ravaged her. Ever since, she's complained of feeling hot all over, as if the fever were allayed but never quenched. I should have burned her copy of the Venetian Cornaro's book! She took its gospel of starvation as a recipe for good health and longevity—a regime that, in Lidian's zeal, turned her into a living skeleton.

"Queenie, forgive me."

She did not hear me or chooses to ignore my feeble atonement. She pokes the ashes with a stick, taking stock of the aftermath of my folly. The ashes still retain a modicum of warmth—as do we two, as do we yet.

Lidian, I forget the warmth you show me, and often give you chilliness in return. We once knew the heat of passion. Or do I mistake?

Wanting to be kind, she says, "Seeing it now through eyes that don't sting from smoke, I'd say the damage is far less than I'd imagined. A petty inferno—nothing more—in contrast to the fire that leaped up onto the roof and brought the slates crashing into the garret."

The Great Fire of July 24, 1872! Our neighbors managed to rescue almost everything. The burly Gregory boys carried Lidian's piano to their parlor. Louisa and her sister May saved nearly all my manuscripts, which, dampened by the fire brigade, they dried on their kitchen stove. I'd have given up the pen for good and gone voluntarily to the asylum had my journals and indices gone up in smoke. They are the organ and refreshment of my memory. When I am stripped of my faculties, like a disgraced general of his decorations, I will be remembered by my leavings.

I join Lidian at the fence and find that, contrary to my expectation, the white pickets are unscorched. Dumbly, I finger the pointed end of one. Is she thinking of the English tea roses that she transplanted from her Plymouth yard? They didn't take to Concord dirt.

"It's easy to imagine an evil agency behind this small desolation."

Laughing good-naturedly, she forbears to say that it was not by any malign intent that the hedge caught fire but, rather, by her husband's befuddlement.

I regard her tenderly. "My mind's bedeviled, old girl."

"The wheel has turned, husband, and we find ourselves—"

"About to be ground to bits."

"Is there no truth in your poems, then? Were you dishonest with yourself when you wrote, 'So nigh is grandeur to our dust, / So near is God to man . . .'?"

"When I went to California with Edith, my mind was already uncertainly arranged."

"Nonsense!"

"I took my hoariest lectures to read at the lyceums in Oakland and San Francisco, in the hope that I'd be less likely to lose my way amid the snakes and ladders of thought. At one given by the 'celebrated natural philosopher R. W. Emerson,' I knocked over a vase of Indian pinks decorating the platform while I was sawing the air, as if I'd never read Hamlet's advice to the players."

Memory is the thread on which the beads of a human life are strung, one by one. Mine snapped, and the beads lay scattered.

"And what did the celebrated Mr. Emerson do to save the situation?"

"He picked up the flowers, stuck them in the vase, and went on, in the way of an old man who, out for a walk in the woods, trips over a Virginia creeper."

"And how did the audience respond?"

"They clapped."

"There!"

"Not in appreciation for the essay. My voice having modulated toward inaudibility, I doubt anyone sitting beyond the first two rows could hear it. No, they clapped because they wished to spare an old man shame and, perhaps, tears."

"Mr. Emerson, I don't care for self-pity!"

"'The things which I have seen I can now see no more.' Wordsworth."

She has rounded on me and gives my frail shoulders a shake. So much fire, I think, for a small old woman, who is seldom without a pain, to remind her that the world is far from ideal.

"When self-reliance is no longer possible, Queenie, self-pity is sure to follow."

"Husband, I won't hear such talk! You've been lucky. The poverty you knew as a young man at Harvard was not the wretched thing I bore as an orphan. You may have dined too often on salt fish and pork scraps; your bowels may have griped you; but you didn't die of lockjaw like poor John Thoreau or lose two legs to Confederate cannonballs like Charles Latham."

"I waged war like a parlor abolitionist—on lecture platforms and with petitions."

"Pity them, not yourself! And you can thank the Lord that age and a bad hip kept you out of that dreadful business."

The angel caught Jacob on his hip and threw him.

"I admit that you suffered a terrible loss—"

Dear Ellen!

"—when your first wife died."

Our bereavements bring us no nearer to God.

"I'm well aware that you spent your allotment of conjugal passion on her."

I pretend to be incensed. "Now who's talking nonsense?"

"I know, I'm plain and sickly."

"Not plain, never plain!"

Margaret Fuller was plain, but one had only to listen awhile to her conversation to think her beautiful. She had an overabundance of animal spirits.

"It seems to me, Queenie, that ever since you took up your poetry again, you've begun to bloom. Nell said the same."

How I wish that the death mask you've worn so long would crack and fall away and I would see you young and fair again!

Lidian ignores the compliment, though I meant it in earnest.

"I hadn't your Ellen's beauty or gaiety."

I dare not accuse Lidian of self-pity, although her voice betrays an emotion that I can't recall ever having sensed in her.

"Ellen had gifts that are sometimes granted to fugitive things," I say, studying my nails. In them, I see the awful truth of our humanity.

When I was a boy dazzled by shells tumbling in the surf, I'd put them in my pocket, only to find, at home, when I took them out again, they had dried into nothing more entrancing than a schoolmaster's stick of chalk.

"I would have been satisfied to live out my days in my own house at Plymouth. But you, Mr. Emerson, would have me for your wife, in spite of my utilitarian . . ."

She finishes her thought by a gesture of resignation to a body that has disappointed her.

A parade of ants defiles through the sere grass, singing, "When the ants come marching home again, Hurrah! Hurrah!" Are they mindless creatures or endued with a common mind? Of the two possible types, which would be the happier and more fulfilled?

"Ours was a happy meeting of the minds, Lidian."

She produces a sound in her throat such as a sparrow would make, beating up the dust with its wings.

Again I blunder, as if, unconsciously, I intend to demolish her. "I admire your passion for reforming society and an intellect that time has not dulled."

She turns her scalding eyes on me. Abashed, I turn mine to the ground, where a fugitive ant staggers onward to its destination, unless it has forgotten it and, withal, its raison d'être.

"You have a great soul, Queenie, and your gray eyes . . ."

Dimmer now.

"Appeared always to see beyond this world."

To the colonnades of eternity, or else the scaffolds of oblivion.

"You were a commissioned spirit."

"I was an ordinary woman—"

"By no means 'ordinary.'"

"A woman who wanted us to live in Plymouth! But you wouldn't hear of it."

"Concord, also, has its rock, and modern pilgrims converge on it."

She wrinkles her nose, as though recoiling at the smell of cabbage in a poor man's hovel.

"I never hoped nor particularly wished to electrify you, Mr. Emerson, but now and again, I'd have liked to arouse an enthusiasm equal to your zeal for the German philosophers."

"Do you remember how I'd sometimes call you 'Asia' because of the mystic continent I perceived in you and the regal manner of your sovereignty?"

I catch a glimpse of Henry walking the roof ridge like a funambulist. I glare, wishing the prat would fall. In his condition, the harm would be only to his pride. I telegraph him through the ether. *"Go away, Henry!"*

Lidian's dyspeptic temper has flared at the mention of "Asia," which I always intended as a compliment.

"I'm not a continent, Mr. Emerson! And I have no illusions regarding my sovereignty, except as it may be over the kitchen, the pantry, and the azaleas."

"When we met, my dear wife, you were a soaring Transcendentalist!"

"My paraffin wings melted long ago. I am what you see."

I need you, Lidian, if for no other reason than to have someone to adore. From adoration, which is reverence, religion springs. I dare not admit to my need for you, because it would only confirm my selfishness. Like a boy who has been scolded, I hang my head and scuffle the dust.

"I'm a fool."

"This day has done much to certify you as one, and it is only half past two."

She goes to the wounded gate.

"Wife, are you going out?"

"'Asia' has errands to run in town. Will you accompany me, or do you intend to hide in your study and sulk like Achilles in his tent at the gates of Troy?"

He *wept* for his friend Patroclus, who was robbed of his wits by Apollo and cut down by Hector with a spear. I could have wept for Henry had I been a Greek instead of a New England scholar.

"Unless you intend to fall on a sharpened paling, you should be safe left on your own for a while."

"I'll go with you. I can't remember when I last walked into town."

"Two days ago, when you took your boots to the cobbler's."

Henry was on his way to Tolman, the shoemaker, when Constable Staples regretfully arrested him for refusing to pay his poll tax. Henry went without a murmur, curious to see what progress our kind has made since the days of Torquemada. Afterward, he wrote, "Under a government which imprisons any unjustly, the true place for a just man is also a prison."

The Tolmans lost a daughter to the asylum. Sometimes I think madness is rampant in Concord, and that I am the maddest of all. I shudder to imagine myself shut away like Bulkeley.

Lidian steps through the gate and onto the Cambridge Turnpike. Feeling momentarily unmanned, I trail after her, in the manner of Hindu wives. I stop to call down the pike to Louisa Alcott, who is chasing dropped red maple leaves in front of her house with a broom. I'd like to hear news of her sister May, the artist of the Alcotts. Ruskin praised her copies of Turner, and her painting *La Négresse* is hanging in the Paris Salon. She painted a panel of goldenrod for my study, which is very fine. Having waved to me and, for the moment, routed the leaves, Louisa goes back inside her house.

Another day, then.

Lidian is well out in front of me on the road to town as I dawdle at my neighbors' horse block. The weathered stones are stained, as though with tears, though I suspect it is the result of horse piss. My brother Charles said—oh, a long time ago—"We are to go forward with freedom until we feel ourselves checked. This check we are never to contend with; when it is right for us to act, it will be removed." What a good and original mind was lost when the poor fellow died!

"Mr. Emerson, are you coming?"

"If it's all the same to you, Queenie, I think I'll turn back."

"As you wish."

"The town will wonder who the old man is hanging on your arm."

A bit of doggerel intended to impress the letter *E* on children's memory sings mockingly in the golden aspen leaves shivering in the nearby schoolyard:

> Emerson was an elephant,
> Stately and wise:
> He had tusks and a trunk,
> And two queer little eyes.
> Oh, what funny small eyes!

Lidian turns her back on me and continues down the pike toward society. She isn't wrong in trying to drive me into communion with my kind. Society is not to be disdained, because it is nature's ultimate form. I see vexation in Lidian's gait, and by the sympathetic resonance of man and wife, her annoyance with me becomes mine with her. My face grows warm, and I'm aware once again that the human heart is flammable.

She calls to me over her shoulder, "Leave the gate for the yardman to fix."

To walk with her to town and back. Why am I so churlish to refuse a small request from one who asks so little of me? An hour on the road and in the stores—what would it cost me, who has nothing to do this afternoon, except to listen to my cells complain and my blood object to its wearisome circuit?

Returning to the yard, I kick the gate and send it flying from its remaining hinge.

"There is a crack in everything!"

Leaning against a chestnut tree, Henry is carving a small horse with his jackknife.

"*Remember the menagerie I made for Edward and little Edith?*"

"*Lidian is unhappy with me.*"

"*You can hardly blame her, Waldo.*"

"*Yet she did say that I'm not to blame for my unraveling mind.*"

"*As I recall, she didn't put it quite that way.*"

"*Well, she said it's not for me to will myself well.*"

He squints at his creation. Isn't it odd that an object should come into greater focus when one's eye is nearly shut? Perhaps only then do we begin to see the thing itself.

"*Philosophy is for bachelors, Waldo. Nature won't reveal herself amid squalling babes, bleating wives, small boys playing with hoops and soldiers, and little girls scolding their dolls. The ponds and trees made no demands on me. Surrounded by them, I was free.*"

He folds up his jackknife and gives me the toy horse. Even in the midst of controversy, I pause to admire it. I wonder at its solidity.

"*Henry, what's that you're nibbling?*"

"*Sugared shagbark hickory meats. I helped myself to a pocketful while the Shakers were whirling, oblivious to everything but God.*"

"*So that's where you went?*"

Though I do love the sweet, I forbear to ask for one, fearful that it may have been altered by vapors of the afterlife shut up in Henry's pocket. He is, I know, indubitably dead; John Muir told me so.

"*Henry, if I should lose both my words and my wife, I won't rest easy in whatever comes next.*"

"*Nothing comes next, save as the living wish it and words make it.*"

"*I thought as much.*"

"*My atoms, however, are ecstatic.*"

"*I'm afraid, Henry, and it shames me to admit it.*"

"*I've seen you face down a pro-slavery mob, which would have done to you what cruel boys do to frogs.*"

"*Did I? I recall Garrison's having done so.*"

"*For a bantamweight, you were uncommonly brave in opposing the bullies of our race.*"

"*But how am I to live bereft of language, which has been my life?*"

"*Hasn't a mute a life?*"

"*Henry, you know very well what I mean! The words are deserting by ones and twos from my brain. There may come a time when they exit in battalions. It's an agony—and yet Lidian rebukes me for self-pity.*"

I look up at the sky, as though I would see my words there like a flight of migrating birds.

"Perhaps language is another veil obscuring the one true fact."

"Language is the universe, Henry, each word a star."

"And even should all the stars fall, how will the one true fact of Ralph Waldo Emerson be changed?"

"Should I thrill to my own dissolution like a child who sees a meteor shower?"

Henry raises a hand, as if intending to conduct the stars in a celestial conflagration.

"Yours would be splendid, Waldo, like the Leonid meteor storm of '33, when a hundred thousand points of light fell every hour of that glorious November night!"

"You overestimate my vocabulary by several orders of magnitude, Henry."

"So long as I don't overestimate the man."

I look at the trees.

"By late November, when the Leonids are once again proclaiming the gaudiness of God, there won't be a leaf left on the trees, at the rate they're dropping."

I kick some leaves that have dropped after I raked and burned their brothers.

"All the better to see the reality of the tree, my friend."

"You may as well say that a man is truly understood only when he's nothing but bones."

"Only then do we clearly see the vanity and illusion of life. Be it life or death, we crave only reality. 'The hand of the Lord was upon me, and carried me out in the spirit of the Lord, and set me down in the midst of the valley, which was full of bones.' Ezekiel."

"Henry, none of this is helpful."

"It's not meant to be. Besides, you don't sound like a man at a loss for words."

"My forgetfulness is in adjournment. There are days—some hours of the day—when I feel my old self. But I know that, little by little, I'm sloughing it off."

"To be reborn as a snake?"

Henry flickers his tongue obscenely—a most un-Henry-like gesture, leaving me, briefly, to wonder if I am talking to a Thoreauvian impostor or the Devil himself, to speak in the old style.

"I'd be satisfied to become a man who knew better, this time round, how to live his life."

"Mr. Emerson, shall we walk?"

Henry and I walk about the yard, his eyes fixed on the ground.

"You won't find any potsherds or arrowheads."

"I believe that if I were to dig deep enough, I'd find woolly mammoth bones."

"Bones again, Henry!"

"Nature undressed and whispering, 'Carpe diem.'"

"Eschatology is a doctrine more readily taken up by callow young divines than elderly men of letters, for whom last things are 'hurrying near.'"

"'And yonder all before us lie / Deserts of vast eternity.' Andrew Marvell."

Henry stands in front of the kitchen window. I hear it answer his knuckled knock. How potent is a mind possessed by an illusion! How easily it resurrects the dead, especially a mind whose cable has been cut. To be visited by a ghost who knocks, whittles, and walks on my rooftop—what a day this is!

"*Do you remember the night Samuel Long threw a stone at your chamber window?*"

"*Was it he? I suspected a Copperhead taking exception to my abolitionism.*"

"*It was an act of defiance, Waldo.*"

I can see how it would be."

"*And a test.*"

"*I don't take your meaning.*"

"*To see how you would behave.*"

"*And how did I behave?*"

"*You shivered in your nightshirt.*"

"*What did he expect?*"

Standing on the mossy stump of an oak tree cut down fifty years ago, Henry gives a fair imitation of me on a lecture platform, reciting one of my verses.

"*He thought you might recite, 'The word unto the prophet spoken / Was writ on tables yet unbroken . . .' or some such Orientalism.*"

"*One cannot always rise to the occasion, especially when wearing a nightshirt.*"

"*There's nothing so purgative as a window shattering in the middle of the night.*"

"*Henry, have you been to Walden Pond lately?*"

"*I like to walk there in the evening, when the sun is low and the depths of the water are revealed. A lake is earth's eye; looking into which the beholder measures the depth of his own nature."*

"Last week, Frank Sanborn caught a seven-pound gold-and-emerald pickerel in your cove."

"Pickerel seem to me as foreign as Arabia to our Concord life, as if the two ends of the earth had come together."

"Our deepest thoughts resemble them."

"Waldo, will we ever be able to think of a pickerel— or a great white whale—not as an evocation of the invisible, but as an animal?"

Henry casts an invisible line, watching as it lofts and then drops at my feet.

"When Radiance shall have burned away the mists of conjecture, there will be no need for poetry—or pickerel, for that matter. Human beings will eat the air."

"There'll be no need for thoughts, either, Mr. Emerson, or carping philosophers to think them."

"Once, I was one of them."

"What are you now, my elderly friend?"

"The blackening sea."

"A drowning man lives until his fire's out."

I fall into the old routine, the scholarly patter that, at times, seems all that's left of youth's heroic days.

"Henry, inasmuch as I breathe, I am."

"And inasmuch as you speak sensibly, you think."

I pick up a stone—a piece of common schist— like a geologist giving a public lecture. *"Until I become as dumb as a stone."*

"Do you suppose stones have nothing to say?" Henry takes the stone from my hand and holds it to his ear. *"They speak in a language older than ours, and when every word is finally lost to you, you may understand, at last, and thereby reach enlightenment."*

I wish to learn this language, not that I may know a new grammar, but that I may read the great book that is written in that tongue.

"Lidian will have something enlightening to say about the broken gate."

"Then fix it, Emerson!"

"You were the mechanic."

"Then I'll instruct you in elementary carpentry."

"God help me!"

Henry takes the willow twig he's been gnawing and studies it as intently as a man would who expects to see God (or the all-consuming fire) in the ardent end of his cigar.

"I doubt the Maker of Days can hang a gate."

Satisfied with his witticism, he puts the twig between his teeth again.

"'The words of the wise are as nails fastened by the master of assemblies.'"

"That's more or less true, Waldo."

I get a hammer, nails, a plumb bob, and some raw lumber from the shed and manage to restore the gate to something of its former condition, sans glory, sans paint. (Asserting a dead man's privilege, Henry didn't lift a finger.)

"Eepur si muove!" I'm pleased with myself as I watch the gate move on its hinges.

"With practice, you'll be able to build a privy."

"And you, Henry, shall be my privy counselor."

I go into the kitchen and pour a mug of beer. Three sharp raps coming from the yard send a shiver down my back. "Here's a knocking indeed!" *Macbeth*, the porter scene. What a joy to be surrounded by one's wits, a sane man's kith and kin! God grant that I shall know them still on the morrow.

I go outside into the dooryard in time to see a black man striking a picket with a stick.

"'Who's there, i' th' name of Beelzebub?'" I shout.

The man takes off his hat. It is stained, as are his sack coat and patched trousers. His boots are worn and dusty. He has the look of someone who has walked the roads and slept in barns—a man on a pilgrimage in a fallen world. He puts me in mind of the ragged Neapolitan beggars I saw during my first trip abroad.

"Mister, is there anything I can do for you to earn the price of a meal? I haven't eaten since yesterday's breakfast."

My own sits heavily on my stomach, like John Calvin's dismal religion or David Hume's skepticism, which, in its extremity, would make the earth stink with suicides.

"I just fixed the gate you're thumping, so, no, I'm

sorry, there's nothing that wants doing. I can give you a little money to be going on with."

Henry tsk-tsks his disapproval from the plum tree he climbed while I was savoring the yeasty taste of ale and the pleasant seething of its foam. At this time of year, plums are few and mostly shrunken or wormy. He, too, is of unsound flesh where he lies a-mouldering. I shudder to picture maggots at their business and shake the thought from my head, as if to evict a troublesome tenant gnat from its lodgings in my ear. What is worse? To be of unsound mind or flesh.

"I've a suit of clothes you can have; I was saving it for my funeral. And a hat that should fit you."

"I'd rather work than accept your charity."

"The kitchen window."

Reflected in the kitchen window, my face reveals the double aspect of my thought—that of the ecstatic idealist Plotinus, who believed in the mystical union of the self with the One, and that of the celebrant of human life Montaigne, who relished each day's earthly good.

"What about it, Henry?"

"Remember Samuel Long."

"Ah, an excellent idea!"

I pick up a stone and throw it. The window shivers, breaks, and shatters the image of my bemused face. Thus by a violent act, the jarring chords that compose the comic operetta that is Ralph Waldo

Emerson are resolved, and he is freed from the Manichean shackles of either/or.

"It sounded very like the crack of doom, my iconoclastic friend."

I turn to my flesh and blood visitor—black flesh and red blood.

"You can fix *that*."

The man stares a moment in astonishment, which turns to doubtfulness, and then to a glower of resentment. "I said no charity, mister!" He puts on his hat and turns to the road.

"I'm old and often at the mercy of caprices over which I have little, if any, control."

To reinforce the impression of senile eccentricity, I do a buck-and-wing.

Up in the tree, Henry laughs and takes a bite of rotten plum.

"For whatever reason, the window is broken and needs to be replaced. Will you do it, or shall I have the carpenter come?"

"I'll do it."

Sullen, he enters the yard. Seen up close, his face looks like seared meat. He regards me with suspicion. I hope to lessen it by the offer of a glass of beer.

"Thank you kindly. I'm parched."

"Come into the kitchen and sit awhile before you start to glaze."

As the stranger and I go into the house, I glance at the plum tree. Henry has gone—to Walden Pond, maybe, to peer into its untroubled depths when the sun descends, or else to heaven to tend his bean field. I must remember to ask if he takes the blessed of the imperial town huckleberrying. When he was at his best—as a man, I mean, of flesh and sinewed bone— he would drop everything to lead a party of young people to search the woods and bogs for the tart fruit that he loved.

I point to a chair, and the stranger sits. I pour him beer and give him a slab of cold meat on a plate, the mustard pot, and half a loaf of bread. As I sweep the shards of broken glass into a corner, he lays into his meal with the single-mindedness of a Roman Catholic supping at the altar rail, devouring the transubstantiated body of Christ. I put the offending stone on the windowsill, in memoriam of action, wondering if I had been rash to cast it and, if so, whether or not it can be salutary to throw caution to the winds.

"I wish I had something else to serve you, but we've lost another cook. Unless we chain the next one to the stove, I fear she, too, will join her many predecessors in deserting us."

He looks up from his meat with something like resentment in his bloodshot eyes, as if he fears that, given half a chance and a moment's inattention, the plate might disappear. Might he sense the unreality in the air, increased by the aromatic quince, which is nowhere present in this house?

I forgive him his wolfish hunger, as one should who himself has never been famished. He finishes the ham and bread, empties the glass, then wipes his mouth on a shabby sleeve. Seeing me regard him with curiosity, he winces, rubs a rough palm across his bristly cheek, and, with a defiant shove, sets the mustard pot skating on the slippery oilcloth. The pot stops just shy of the table edge, like a lucky shuffleboard disk. I sigh to think of what tawny outrage might have been done to Lidian's floor had the kitchen god or a bit of grit in the cogs of fate not intervened on my behalf.

"No harm done."

"Mister, I wasn't always rude and cussed, but an ill wind can peel the veneer off a man, like paint from a barn."

"Good manners are made up of petty sacrifices. I could probe you to the marrow, I think, and find only grave matters."

"If it's not a waste of breath to say I've had my share of troubles, then I'll say it."

"You'll find me a sympathetic listener, if you care to tell your story, Mr. . . ."

"Stokes."

"Mr. Stokes, I bid you welcome to Bush. Please make yourself at home."

"You don't happen to have any tobacco, do you, friend?"

"If you'd fancy a cigar, I'll join you in a smoke."

"I would, thank you kindly."

I take two Havana cigars from the case inside my vest. Having lighted his, he sits back in his chair and contemplates the live coal of tobacco that his match has brought into being. He eyes me next with equal interest, as though he expects me to combust. When I don't, he draws up to the table, coughs, and fidgets with his cigar, like someone getting up the nerve to make a clean breast of what weighs heavily there.

In a polished platter, I watch as my features assemble into the face of a confessor whose heart, I hope, is charitable. "My son, is there something you wish to tell me?"

"Maybe."

"While you make up your mind, we'd better get the window fixed, or the magpies will be looting my wife's sewing basket."

It isn't a magpie that puts its head in the empty window frame, but Lidian, who cocks her head, birdlike, to take in the damage.

"Mr. Emerson, what have you done now?"

I consider the consequences of a truthful answer and decide to lie. "Billy Spicer threw a stone at the plum tree and missed."

"That boy is beyond redemption!"

"He wanted to knock Henry from his perch."

She doesn't even bother to remind me that Henry Thoreau is, in the common meaning of the word, *dead*. She sniffs through her thin nose, shrugs her bony shoulders, and announces her intention to visit our married daughter, Edith, on Naushon Island, in Buzzards Bay, before Sam Staples arrests her for the murder of the chief ornament of the age—R. W. Emerson.

I think it an excellent idea and tell her so, wishing that she would hurry.

"The Boston train leaves at four and connects with the New Bedford line at half past six. Will and Edith will take me across in the *Gypsy*."

I clear my throat and swing my chin toward the black man.

"Mr. Emerson, I see you have company."

I'm glad to have his reality confirmed by other than the smear of mustard on his plate.

"Mrs. Emerson, allow me to introduce Mr. . . ."

Having forgotten his name, I fall into an embarrassed silence. Each such stumble is a stone laid on the grave of memory.

He introduces himself. "Stokes. James Stokes."

"Mr. Stokes, if you'll excuse me, I must pack my grip and cannot stop to talk. But my husband is in a garrulous mood today, even if his interlocutors are figments of his impetuous imagination."

Stokes smiles strangely, and I feel uneasy once again.

Lidian flies up the stairs. After a commotion of drawers and closets, she reappears before us, dressed in traveling clothes and a poke bonnet. Carrying a hastily packed valise, she does not pause in her headlong flight toward the depot, except to enjoin me to fix the window. She leaves nothing in her wake, except the scent of pears, which winter at the bottom of her closet, together with her summer shoes.

Like a thirsty horse searching the air for water, I sniff and guess which variety of pear perfumed my wife's departure.

Say the pretty words, Waldo, if only in your mind: *Louise Bonne de Jersey, Flemish Beauty, Easter Beurré*, plain but reliable *Bartlett*. Golden words for golden fruit! I taste them in my mouth.

"I hope she didn't leave on my account, Mr. Emerson."

"The account is all mine, friend."

"A fine woman, from what I saw of her."

"She has a bee in her bonnet. Lately, it is often so."

"Then she'd better find the kitchen window fixed when she gets back."

"Mr. Stokes, you're right. Left to myself, I'd spend the remainder of the daylight hours in dithering."

I show him where panes and putty are kept, in anticipation of storms and boyish mischief.

"Do your work, and I shall know you."

Soon, he has sealed the house against hungry squirrels, marauding birds, and crickets wanting to winter by the hearth.

"Thank you, Mr. Stokes."

"Thank you, sir, for the supper and cigar."

As he gets into his tattered coat, I notice he is bleeding.

"Why, you've cut your arm on the glass!"

"Don't worry yourself, Mr. Emerson."

He manages to bind the wound with a handkerchief, knotting it fast with his strong teeth. In a moment, the blood seeps through it. How very red is his blood!

When Samuel Long cut his finger fixing the cucumber frame, my daughter Nelly was surprised by the color of his blood. She thought it would be black, a childish belief shared by many in their majority and no less preposterous than the so-called science of craniometrics, espoused by university anatomist Dr. Samuel George Morton in his book *Crania Americana*: "Racial intellectual capacity can be determined by measuring interior cranial capacity."

"Mr. Stokes, you need medical attention."

"Mister, I don't care for doctors."

"I fear you won't care much for the alternative."

I lead him back into the kitchen and make him sit.

"Elevate the wound above your heart, James, while I fetch my neighbor Miss Alcott, who is something of a nurse."

His lips purse in derision. In a sedate town like ours, he doubtless imagines that Miss Alcott will be acquainted with the magistrate's lumbago, the banker's gout, the indelicacies of childbirth, and deaths by natural causes—unpleasant odors concealed beneath the scents of talc and lilac water. What can a genteel woman of Concord know of a black man's wounds?

"She learned her trade at Union Hospital in Georgetown during the war. She nursed sick and wounded soldiers till she caught typhoid fever and was brought home in an appalling state."

I glance to see what effect Louisa May's dedication to the cause of his emancipation has on Stokes, but his face is a blank. Do I expect him to show gratitude—insist on it, even?

What a fellow you've turned out to be, Emerson! What a hypocrite!

"Before the war, Miss Alcott was a conductor of the Underground Railroad."

Please, Mr. Stokes, do not sneer!

He smiles—a trifle tight-lipped, perhaps.

"I'll be grateful to Miss Alcott."

I hurry along the pike and, having informed Louisa of the matter, she returns with me, carrying a box, such as ladies' hats are kept in, which proves to be filled with what is needed to stitch, to staunch, to stave off death awhile.

How strange it is to recall that Margaret Fuller, our impassioned diva, tended mutilated soldiers of the Roman Republic when the ancient city was assailed by monarchists, papists, and French troops sent by

King Louis Napoléon to put Pope Pius IX back on Saint Peter's rock! Try as I may, I cannot picture her amid the cots of the Ospedale Fatebenefratelli—tearing, with her teeth, strips of cloth from her dress to bind a man's wounds.

Louisa inspects Stokes's arm. "It'll need to be stitched. Do you keep whiskey in the house, Mr. Emerson?"

Although I exhort my fellow men to "drink the wild air," I keep a bottle or two of ardent spirits for company. I give one to her. She takes a sip to steel herself, pours a little on the man's wound—a libation that makes him mutely wince—then gives him the bottle to nurse while she readies the needle.

"All right, Mr. Stokes?"

"Yes, ma'am."

As she expertly sews the gash, I feel my face blanch and step into the dooryard to distract myself with the recent history of the chickens, written in a twiggy alphabet imprinted on the dust. Once more the master of myself, I go back inside as Louisa finishes dressing Stokes's wound.

"All done!"

"I appreciate the kindness, Miss Alcott."

"Not at all, Mr. Stokes. I'm happy to have helped."

"I'm sorry I can't pay you."

"Nonsense! I did what any Christian would do."

Or Hindu, Jew, Mohammedan, Confucian, or Zoroastrian . . .

"I'm just along the pike, if you should need me again."

She washes her hands at the sink, then packs her hatbox.

"Thank you, my dear."

"I've soup bones for Lidian. I'll bring them later."

"She's fled Egypt to spend a night or two with Edith and the children."

Louisa's face registers surprise, as well it might, since Lidian is often ill. Or does she consider me too incompetent to be left on my own?

"Lately, she's been a dynamo that Michael Faraday himself would admire."

I myself am full of admiration for Lidian's decisiveness, a quality many times absent from philosophers and old men—especially this elderly scholar, who can no longer distinguish between the resolute and the rash.

I follow Louisa into the yard.

"Waldo, is Mr. Stokes someone known to you?"

"No, he just turned up at the backyard gate."

"You should be careful of strangers who just turn up."

"He is not, as I feared, the devastator of the day. Nor do I believe he has designs on the family silver." I pick up a stick and thrust it at her as Tybalt did Mercutio. "Zounds!"

"Waldo! You're not yourself!"

Chastened, I return to my visitor in the kitchen, dragging the stick behind me.

"Where are you heading, Mr. Stokes?"

"I want to get up into Canada."

"Canada, you say."

"I'm a runaway, Mr. Emerson."

Suddenly, it is not James Stokes sitting opposite me at the kitchen table, but Samuel Long on the evening that Alcott brought him here. Samuel had run away from a Tidewater plantation and, under the Fugitive Slave Act, was liable to arrest and return to his owner, Charles Jeroboam. I offered Samuel an unused cabin in Walden Woods, in exchange for keeping a watchful eye on Henry.

"Samuel, are you dead? Did they lynch you, too, from the magnolia tree?"

Samuel raises his head, so that I can see the livid bruise on his throat left by the noose.

"I'm sorry."

"So am I, Waldo, so am I."

"You were a good man."

"Mr. Emerson, are you all right?"

"Mr. Stokes, I am. Why do you ask?"

"You're talking to yourself."

"A habit for which my wife never tires of reproving me. Forgive me, James, but in my old age, I enjoy the company of familiars—some dead, others living elsewhere. While it can dismay onlookers, it is a comfort to me. Perhaps you should tell me what you're running from."

"The army."

"The Union's or the Confederacy's?"

"There's only the United States Army now. The War of the Rebellion has been over for fourteen years."

"Yes, of course it has. You must forgive an old man his lapses."

"I fought in the last battle of the war, at Palmito Ranch, in Brownsville, Texas, with the Sixty-second Regiment of U.S. Colored Troops. I got this at Tulosa Bluff from a rebel mortar shell."

He shows me a scar beneath the rib cage. It reminds me of a knot on a blackthorn tree, whose branches are favored by witches for broomsticks to fly on and by old men to lean upon in their decrepitude.

"I am faithful, I do not give out, / The fractur'd thigh, the knee, the wound in the abdomen, / These and more I dress with impassive hand . . ."

"Whitman, are you here, too?"

I feel in the thin air; I poke it with my stick.

"We lost plenty of men in the thickets along the Rio Grande and to Colonel Ford's attack during our retreat to Boca Chica, after we'd burned the rebel supplies at Palmito Ranch. Some drowned in the river while the Mexicans and French fired on us from the opposite bank."

"Emerson, I am here and everywhere."

"Lord, what a crowded day it's been!"

"It was for nothing, goddamn it! The Confederacy was done for: Lee had surrendered the Army of Northern Virginia to Grant. Mr. Lincoln was dead, and Jeff Davis on the run, dressed in his wife's old shawl. But 'Rip' Ford wasn't about to surrender to niggers, Tejanos, and savages—'perfidious renegades,' he called us. And he sure as hell wasn't going to let a fortune in Mifflin Kenedy cotton, sitting baled and pretty on a Brownsville wharf, fall into Union hands! He intended to send it across the Rio Grande. Ford planned to be a rich Mexican *patrón*."

"Yes, it is often that way when money is to be made."

"Swindlers, shysters, spoilsmen, assassins, I admonish you—I bid you take heed!"

"Whitman, come out and show yourself!"

"Does seem like it." Stokes buttons his shirt and tucks it into his trousers.

Less quick than Henry, Garrison, Louisa, and Lidian to declare myself an abolitionist, I dare not ask Stokes if he was, in his younger days, another man's property. His response might sting my conscience. (Conscience is an open wound that, having scabbed over, becomes callus.) I waited till the summer of '44 to come out of the parlor. I don't recall why I hesitated, unless it was that I heard the wary voice of Hamlet, who tenants every overly thoughtful brain, urging me to wait until doubt could be completely overthrown by evidence.

How we humans like to mollify our guilty consciences, as burns are commonly buttered to salve them! The result of this homely remedy is to fry the injured skin.

🌲

Stokes follows me into my study.

"You were saying, Mr. Stokes, before we were interrupted?"

He doesn't turn a hair at my remark, which others might find curious.

"After the war, I joined the Ninth Cavalry, Company L, called 'Buffalo Soldiers' by the Cheyenne because of the robes we wore in winter on the plains and our black crimped hair and beards. In December 1877, we were ordered to El Paso after the uprising at San Elizario."

He tells me about the five hundred "Tejanos," as the subjugated Mexicans of Texas are called, who captured twenty Texas Rangers sent by the governor to back the claim of big-bug Democrat Charles Howard to the salt that the *saltieros* of San Elizario had been gathering ever since the king of Spain granted them the immense dry salt lake. Salt was their livelihood and the currency used to barter up and down El Camino Real de Tierra Adentro, the sixteen-hundred-mile road from Santa Fe to Mexico City. By the federal Treaty of Guadalupe Hidalgo, concluded in 1848 to our advantage after the United States Army seized vast tracts of northern Mexico, the Tejanos were guaranteed their salt beds in perpetuity. The new Texas constitution, however, recognized Howard and his cronies' claim to them. For West Texas capitalists, salt is as profitable as wheat wrangled in the trading pits of Chicago.

Listening to Stokes, I recall attending a meeting of the Bible Society of St. Augustine, Florida, while slaves were being auctioned in the yard outside. One ear heard the glad tidings while the other was regaled with "Going, gentlemen, going!"

As though he also hears a black slave knocked down by an auctioneer's hammer, Stokes is angry. He picks up a paper knife on the desk and twirls its point on his palm. Fascinated, I wait to see what he will do. He puts down the knife and continues his story of American chicanery.

"Howard wanted San Elizario's salt not only to sell to gringo beef packers but also to the owners of the Chihuahua mines, who use it to separate silver from its ore. The Tejanos shot him, hacked his body into pieces, and threw them down a well."

"Which will nevermore be sweet."

"Resist much, obey little."

Whitman again!

"Damn you!" I meant to blast the bard in my mind, but the words escaped my mouth.

Stokes glares at me. How easily he could crush my windpipe and put an end to the futile production of words that have done little, if anything, to ameliorate the suffering of the world!

"I was speaking to someone else."

His eyes hunt the air of my study and settle on May Alcott's goldenrod, which calms him.

Knock, knock.

I sent a blistering letter to President Van Buren when he ordered the last of the Cherokee Nation removed from their towns, farms, schools, businesses, and the chambers of their congress to the west side of the Mississippi River, thereby breaking, for the twenty-eighth time, a treaty guaranteeing them the use and perpetual enjoyment of their ancient tribal lands—the portion left to them, that is. Van Buren did not deign to answer. I could do no more.

"Mr. Stokes, I could do no more!"

Knock, knock.

"Someone's at the door."

My words would have been better spent writing valentines and whispering endearments in poor Queenie's ears than in speaking truth to men who have little time for it. Emerson, you're the arch deceiver of yourself to think you've come anywhere near the truth in your forty-odd years of lecturing and lucubrating!

"Odd indeed!"

"Mr. Emerson, somebody's knocking at your front door!"

Knock, and it shall be opened unto you.

With a shake of my head, I break the gossamer of thought in which I've been entangled. I go into the front room and open the door, to find a man weighed down by paper sacks standing on the sill.

"Evening, Mr. Emerson, I've brought your groceries."

"Groceries . . ."

"Mrs. Emerson stopped at the store this afternoon before getting on the Boston train."

"I'll be obliged to you, Lyman, if you'll put them on the kitchen table."

Having done so, he lingers by the front door. Thinking he is waiting for a gratuity, I find a five-cent piece in my pocket.

"Mrs. Emerson already gave me something for my trouble, though it ain't no trouble at all. It's an honor to bring you your groceries, Mr. Emerson, and it's a shame you don't get into town more. You're missed." He steals a glance at Stokes, who has come into the room. "You got company, so I'll be going."

"Mr. Stokes, be acquainted with Mr. Bierce, who supplies the town with necessaries."

The men eye each other like a pair of rival cats lusting for a robin, or two robins for a fat bloodworm in the grass. Be it high or low, we all have our gazes fixed on something choice.

"If memory serves, you have a brother who looks after the town's deceased."

"George. He's a gravedigger at Sleepy Hollow, amongst other things."

"'Amongst other things' comprehends a universe of human endeavor. George might be a grocer of grave goods, for instance, if the trade runs in the family, or a grave robber, like 'Big Jim' Kennally, who, not long ago, conspired to dig up Mr. Lincoln's bones from the Springfield cemetery. They'd fetch a king's ransom, don't you think, Lyman?"

"George is my brother-in-law, to tell the truth. Well, I've got to close up the store. Glad to see you looking fit, Mr. Emerson, and I'm pleased to have made your acquaintance, Mr.—"

"Stokes."

"Mr. Stokes. I'll say good night, then."

I close the door behind the grocer as Stokes pokes at an ottoman with the toe of his boot.

"That fella reminds me of a Tennessee polecat."

Lyman Bierce does have a furtive aspect.

"Earlier, you said you were a fugitive from the army. Would you care to elaborate?"

"I don't know, Mr. Emerson. Somehow, you don't seem in your right mind."

"People who claim to be in their right minds often do the most harm."

My remark was an empty witticism that Henry would have belittled, but it appears to have satisfied Stokes.

"Last month I rode into El Paso, stabled my horse, had a bath, got my hair cut, my beard tidied, and my cowhide boots mended. It was a pleasure to get out of my army clothes and walk the streets, even if I was obliged to bathe and barber in 'nigger town.'

"I was passing a saloon when a corporal of the Fifteenth Infantry—I didn't know him, excepting by his stripes—came out through the swinging doors. He took me by my back collar, spun me round, spat a gob of brown juice in my face, and told me, 'Get your black ass off the sidewalk.' I hit him hard enough to hear his jawbone crack. A soldier jumped from a sutler's wagon and started laying into me with a mule skinner's whip. That's how I come to have this."

He traces a scar from below his ear to the collarbone. Stokes is a traveling exhibition of ill usage suitable for a lyceum platform.

"I took hold of the lash, and before I knew what happened, I'd choked the life out of the son of a bitch."

"I suppose it would have done no good to explain yourself to the authorities."

"You don't know much about the army, do you, Mr. Emerson, or being a negro, for that matter? When a black man kills a white one, there's hell to pay, and the negro pays it. So while the good people of El Paso were hunting up a rope, I got my horse and lit out of there. I rode the poor animal till it wore out, and I've been riding myself till I'm dead on my feet."

"Mr. Stokes, why don't you stop here tonight? There's an unused bed. There's no one but the two of us. You won't be disturbed."

"I would like to bed down in someplace other than a thicket, woods, or barn—I surely would, Mr. Emerson, if it won't put you out."

"Not at all.

"I appreciate the kindness."

♣

I take Stokes upstairs to one of the empty rooms, fill the washbowl, set out soap, a clean cloth, and towel. Having come, at last, to rest, he sinks suddenly into himself. His shoulders sag; his hands hang at his sides. He is like a clock whose mainspring has unwound. I turn down the quilt on the bed in which Margaret Fuller used to sleep when she visited Bush. (The room she stayed in is gone, as is she—one to fire, the other to the sea.) Once, she stopped here for forty days, like Jesus among the wild beasts of the desert, though it was only Jeoffry who showed her his claws. During her visit, Lidian was invalided by an infected jawbone, followed by nervous fever consequent to her broken heart. That was the year of grieving for little Waldo. The day he would have turned six, Lidian went to her sickbed. Like one of the angels who ministered to the Lamb of God in the wilderness, Margaret kept my demons at bay.

"Flights of angels sing thee, Mr. Stokes. Flights of angels."

As I'm about to close the door, I recollect a dream I had one night when I was a divinity student. "I dreamed I ate the world. An angel gave it to me in the guise of an apple. From then on, the world was inside me."

Stokes's brown eyes flash dangerously.

"Did it have nigger slaves in it, the world you swallowed?"

Baffled and hurt, I return his angry look for as long as I dare.

"Maybe you spat them out like pips."

"We're all slaves to time, Stokes. Death puts the iron collar on our necks as soon as we are born."

He must find my remark comical, because he laughs until he wheezes.

"I'd despise you if you tried to curry favor, but the courtesy due your host would not be taken amiss."

"Mr. Emerson, suh, I do begs your pardon."

Without another word, I leave the room, closing the door behind me.

Ah, well, Emerson. It was the same with Samuel Long when he first arrived in Concord. Their consciousness has been shaped by quite different circumstances than any you have known.

Downstairs, I sit at the table and try to make headway on a poem begun in February.

> Outside is winter.
> Except for a Calvary
> Of masts on the river
> And the useless spires,
> The town is vanishing
> In snow as am I.

I haven't managed to extend the piece by so much as a word. I sigh and put the scrap of paper back into the drawer. If a poem could grow in the dark, as eyes do on potatoes! If I could see with the clarity I once possessed! What might the scientific instruments of the future reveal to our astonished eyes? Belial lording it over the animalcules in a drop of stagnant water or "the proud seat of Lucifer" erected beyond the rings of Saturn? Not now, not yet. As Keats said, "But here there is no light."

"Too much light spoils the daguerreotype."

"As does too little."

I turn and see Walt Whitman coming down the stairs. In his gait, I detect evidence of the stroke that stopped him in his tracks, if only for a time. Like an oak half killed by lightning, he'll stand awhile longer in the dooryard singing his peculiar songs. He makes himself comfortable in the overstuffed chair. He takes off his soft hat.

"Walt, what in God's name are you doing?"

"*I sit and look out upon all the sorrows of the world, and upon all oppression and shame, / I hear secret convulsive sobs from young men at anguish with themselves, remorseful after deeds done . . .*"

"*Always the poseur!*"

He shakes a fist at me.

"*I'd knock you on your bony ass, Emerson, but the exertion would kill us both.*"

I try to muster sufficient moisture to spit; lacking juice, however, I manage only dribble, which hangs on my chin.

"*I hope you didn't wake Stokes with your yawping?*"

He scratches his shaggy beard.

"*He sleeps like the dead.*"

"*You should know, you old cuss.*"

"*I'm not dead; I'm in Camden—or I was before I sent my spirit out to beard you in your den, old man.*"

"*You seem more than usually hostile tonight, Walt.*"

"*I'm one hostile who can't be persuaded, bribed, or forced onto the reservation. During a lecture of yours, you said of me that 'he belongs yet to the fire clubs, and has not got into the parlors.'*"

"*Who told you that?*"

"*John Trowbridge. I suppose he's another of your young geniuses.*"

"*Since when have you cared a hangnail for parlors? Isn't Pfaff's beer cellar more to your taste?*"

"*I resent your disparagements, Emerson. I deserve a*

*seat at the high table of literature. I've earned it! I'm too
old to be a writer of promise, perched on a barstool."*

Weary, I sit in this chair, which is as straight-
backed as a young man's principles. I am, however,
no longer young and have grown tired of all the fret
and fritter.

"Walter, I've no time to spare for ancient grudges."

He returns his hat to his head, and with a thumb,
he insolently cocks it.

*"The right man comes—the right hour; the leaf is
lifted."*

He opens his wallet and removes a piece of
yellowed paper nearly worn to pieces from being
unfolded and folded so often since I sent it to him
nearly a quarter century ago. And now the old blus-
terer begins to read it back to me!

> *"'I am not blind to the worth of the won-
> derful gift of* Leaves of Grass. *I find it the
> most extraordinary piece of wit and wisdom
> that America has yet contributed. I am very
> happy in reading it, as great power makes
> us happy. It meets the demand I am always
> making of what seemed the sterile and
> stingy nature, as if too much handiwork or
> too much lymph in the temperament were
> making our Western wits fat and mean. I
> give you joy of your free and brave thought.
> I have great joy in it. I find incomparable
> things said incomparably well, as they must*

*be. I find the courage of treatment, which so
delights us, and which large perception only
can inspire. I greet you at the beginning of a
great career, which yet must have had a long
foreground somewhere for such a start.'*

"Et cetera, et cetera."

Walt carefully folds the letter, and, as he gives me a mischievous wink, he kisses the paper and returns it to his wallet.

"Well, Waldo, what do you have to say for yourself?
Respondez! Respondez!"

*"That I've lived to regret my initial enthusiasm. It
has worn thin—as thin as that piece of writing paper."*

"Without enthusiasm, what is a man?"

*"Your work strikes me as that of a poet not yet fully
grown, albeit 'The Wound Dresser' and 'When Lilacs Last
in the Dooryard Bloom'd' are very fine. They show a man
annealed by immense sorrow—a genuine pity that has
saved you from being seen merely as a chronicler of facts."*

*"What would you have me do, Emerson? Poke among
the veils with a eunuch's sapless wand?"*

*"Your verses can seem like an exordium of declara-
tions and assertions that awaken in me sentiments better
suited to needlepointed mottoes for a parlor wall."*

Walt stands and rolls up a sleeve.

"Whitman, we're too old for fisticuffs!"

*"But not too old for a contest of strength—you and I
being about equally feeble."*

He sits beside me and plants an elbow on the table.

"I mean to arm-wrestle you, you lily-livered school-marm. See if I don't make you cry, 'Uncle'!"

"You've already had two strokes, you 'mere white curd of ass's milk,' to quote Alexander Pope."

"You mealymouthed pedant!"

"A third will carry you off."

"You can roll me up in your Turkey carpet and carry me out death's door, so long as you take back your insults!"

"Damn you, Whitman!"

"Emerson, take them back!"

"I will do no such thing! I sent Carlyle a copy of your 1856 edition and invited him to light his pipe with it."

"Fight me."

"No!"

"Coward."

I sigh, already defeated. His eyes are hectic, his lips curled in a sneer. Even at sixty, he appears formidable, a type of Jeremiah or Ezekiel. I feel about as hearty as Ichabod Crane.

I roll up my sleeve and grip his hand in mine. The veins in our arms push through the skin; the old blood moves according to the tired heart's impulse. The muscles in Walt's arm are stringy; mine seem to have preceded me into the grave.

"On the count of ten, professor . . . One little Indian, two little Indians, three little Indian boys."

He pulls my arm down onto the table with sufficient force to startle the unfinished poem.

"Ho ho!"

"You jumped the gun, Walt!"

"Don't be such a namby-pamby puritan!"

He slaps the tabletop and offers me a second
chance.

I struggle awhile, and then, struck by the lunacy
of this engagement of old men, I let him have his
way. My knuckles thump. Walt beams in triumph,
scratches his beard with all his nails, throws back his
massive head, and laughs as boys do who have been
caught acting foolishly and hope to brave it out.

"We're too old for this horseshit, Waldo!"

"Walter, would you care for a drink?"

I lay my hand lightly on his sleeve as I did at Boston Common nearly twenty years ago, when I tried
to convince him to take the sex out of "Children of
Adam."

"I never say no to a stiff one."

I get the bottle of Kentucky whiskey that I stock
for Ellery Channing. On second thought, the cheap
rye I keep to warm the man who shovels snow is good
enough for nature's roughneck sitting at my table, as
"Exalté, rapt, extatic" as he was in his brawling days.

He fills our glasses, lifts his, and in the voice he
raised at Paumanok against the Atlantic's imperial
roar, he salutes democracy. We go on to toast the
States, the territories, Lincoln, Grant, our mothers,

and the martyr John Brown, whose body and truth lie a-mouldering in the ground.

The bottle, like the miraculous jug at Cana, is apparently inexhaustible.

I'm waiting for my head to split, eyes to blur, tongue to thicken, and words to stagger, but Providence appears to have delivered us from drunkenness—a further miracle to ponder, in a day whose strangeness tomorrow I will be happy to forget.

Walt puffs out his chest and declaims:

> "*O Libertad—turn your undying face,*
> *To where the future, greater than all the past,*
> *Is swiftly, surely preparing for you.*"

We listen to its echo fade away to a sigh, which is always a prelude to silence.

"*O past! O happy life! O songs of joy!*" He wipes a string of drool from his lip. "*When a man arrives at his life's summit, he longs for a comfortable chair and a glass of something to fortify himself against the . . .*"

"*Against what, Walt?*"

"*What is missing from* Leaves of Grass."

"*I thought it contained every last atom and morsel of creation.*"

"*That's the great boast, my dear Emerson, and the great cheat.*"

He musters himself; he assumes his former swagger. I suppose that he has embarrassed himself in front of his old teacher.

"Poor bastard, I heard your mind is unraveling."

"Who told you that?"

"Bronson Alcott.

Ingrate!

"I wouldn't care overmuch about becoming infirm if only my mind were not so. Can you imagine anything more pathetic than a philosopher who can no longer think?"

"A poet who can no longer write because his hands shake and his bleary eyes are filled with rheum."

To cheer him, I try my hand at bravado. *"There are enough knots left at the end of our ropes for us to hold on awhile longer!"*

His grizzled countenance opens in a smile. It warms me, and I return it from my own pallid, closely shaved one. Together, we share a moment of goodwill stripped of pretense and ambition.

"Waldo, have you written anything new?"

"An order for groceries in Whitmanesque fashion, though not with the bard's 'courage of treatment, which so delights us, and which large perception only can inspire.'"

"The muse is only sleeping, my friend; she hasn't yet deserted you."

"Walt, somehow it doesn't seem important any longer."

"You might as well say that the sea is of no importance, or the firmament of stars. Poetry is the Radiance that remains after creation's first day. The faint echo of that awful roar."

"*I think that what's asleep upstairs is beyond all poetry and philosophy.*"

"*You mean the colored fugitive.*"

"*I mean a man who happens to be a negro and a fugitive.*"

I blush to hear myself. Why must we be embarrassed by our better nature?

"*I'm not sure I know what to do with him. Henry would know, but he's gone back to the hollow.*"

Walt goes to the window and gazes at the night. He speaks of a self buried underneath all his boasts of perfect equanimity: "*I love to lie abed on a winter's night when the house is quiet, and there's not a beetle in the wall or a cricket in the closet to disturb the felted stillness. At times, the blab of the pavement, the shouts in the street, my ceaseless yawping make me wish I'd been born deaf and mute and could attend to nothing except the silent progress of souls.*"

"*Sometimes I swear I can hear the yeast in Lidian's bread dough shriek!*"

"*The sourdough eaten with a bitter herb—this, too, is the bread of life.*"

"*A jackass of an editor at the* Bloomington Pantagraph *called me 'Ralph Cold-Dough Simmerson.'*"

"*To think of the ink and breath we two have spent!*"

"*My purse and I wheeze.*"

"*Emerson, you wrote too damned much!*"

He sits. We face each other across the table, two old men at the end of their powers.

"*You, as well, with your thickening mulch. What is a book if not a heap of nouns and verbs enclosing an intuition or two?*"

"'*The rest is silence.*' Shakespeare."

"'*Silence is the element in which great things fashion themselves together; that at length they may emerge, full-formed and majestic, into the daylight of Life, which they are thenceforth to rule.*' Carlyle."

"'*Silence is what follows the last thump of earth on the coffin lid and the great feed at the funeral lunch.*' John Doe."

In such an atmosphere as we two have produced, cakes and kingdoms fall.

Walt looks into my pale blue eyes and apprehends me with his sad gray ones. They have seen much of the world and, through the lens of ecstatic vision, may have descried places where the questing spirit roves unhindered, such as the Mountains of the Moon and the red mountains of Madagascar, the beautiful bay of Nagasaki, the pharaohs' Egypt, and the Pleiades. I almost reach out my hand to touch his, but something prevents me—fear, I suppose, that he will take hold of mine. I sigh, regretting the distance I have kept from others of my kind and from this man, the poet whose coming I foretold. Whitman is our Rabelais, whose Gargantua supped on Christian pilgrims mixed in salads, and also our Pantagruel strutting brazenly in his codpiece.

Walt, you are the full belly of democracy, rank

and ruddy in your fireman's red flannel undershirt, your trousers tucked into your boots. You are gross and coarsely vernacular—and tender withal. You are, as you wrote of yourself at the beginning of your great career, "Walt Whitman, an American, one of the roughs, a kosmos, / Disorderly fleshy and sensual . . . eating drinking and breeding."

He slaps the table with a fleshy palm, scrapes back his chair with an insolent disregard for Lidian's floor, and heaves up his great bulk, insisting that we visit Nathaniel Hawthorne's grave.

"As long as I'm here, I should pay my respects. I won't be coming back to Concord."

"I didn't think you cared much for his books."

"I don't; they have an unwholesome odor of corruption and disease, like Edgar Poe's tales. Their morbidity subverts the democratic optimism I promulge."

I wince at the pompous word.

"I'd have thought the late war had taught you otherwise."

"I have witness'd the true lightning, I have witness'd my cities electric, / I have lived to behold man burst forth, and warlike America rise . . ."

"'For by stroking of him I have found out electricity,'" I say, thinking of our cat Jeoffry, whose literary antecedent was conceived in a London asylum by the mad poet Christopher Smart.

"Will you go with me, Emerson, old chuck?"

I glance at the mantel clock. *"It's gone nine, and the night air will do neither of us any good."*

"Don't be a fuddy-duddy!"

Again, I look at the clock.

"You were always too cautious by half, Waldo."

Vain septuagenarian! I've no wish to seem a pygmy beside this ruined colossus. I put on my coat and hat and wrap my throat in a muffler. I open the front door and nod toward Whitman. Wearing his old hat, baggy pants, and flannel coat, he stands in the doorway, relishing the night beyond and the tonic air.

I'm about to offer him something warmer to put on, when I check myself, realizing that he is only a projection of my need to be again in his company. A magic lantern slide. How perverse human wishes often are!

"After you, old ruffian."

Do I imagine that he pauses to consider the matter of the lintel? It is too low to allow a man of his height to pass without taking off his hat. But Whitman will not doff his hat, bow, or bend a knee to anyone or anything. He leans his big head forward a little, pretends to scratch the back of his neck, and walks out the door, his hat on his head, his pride and purpose intact.

Once again it is proved: A man can walk upright if he but lean a little toward the common center.

I shut the door behind us. We start up Cambridge

Pike, which leads to Concord and, just beyond it on Bedford Street, Sleepy Hollow Cemetery.

I feel a cold sufficient to freeze the ink in Concord inkwells and turn my pages to snow.

II

We are parlor soldiers. We shun the rugged
battle of fate, where strength is born.

—Ralph Waldo Emerson,
"Self-Reliance," 1841

WALT AND I PASS THROUGH a pair of wrought-iron gates. Were the cold night a summer's day, and the rimy grass green and living, and the dead lilies drooping in bronze urns blooming asphodels, I might persuade myself that we have arrived at the Elysium Fields instead of a burying place, the end of all human dreams and philosophies. But it is grocer Bierce's brother-in-law, George Hammond, who tends the graves here and not the titan Kronos.

Crouching behind a willow tree, we watch Hammond wending amid the monuments. He carries a lamp against the darkness, which has fallen over Middlesex County, and an ear trumpet. He stops by each marble and granite remembrance and, getting to his knees, as if to do reverence to the ranks of the

Concord dead, he cocks his head and strains to hear, perchance, a subterranean noise through the instrument's embouchure.

"Waldo, what's he doing?"

"He's listening."

"To what?"

"The maggots that thin the animal, so that it can pass through Pilgrim's wicket-gate."

"What sound do you suppose a maggot makes?"

"One too faint for an ear trumpet, although I expect that if it were amplified a thousandfold, it would remind us of a fire ravenously gnawing wood or a star roaring like a Bessemer."

"In other words, the sound of uncontrollable appetite."

"Yes, Walt, the noise and clamor of it."

"The rude song at the end of the world."

"The song of the States and territories."

I have mocked him, and he glares at me. I wait for him to roll up his sleeve and plant an elbow on a gravestone, but he lets the remark pass. I would take it back, but insults cannot be recanted, any more than a murder can be undone.

"Do you remember your Hamlet? The graveyard scene?"

"'How long will a man lie i' the earth ere he rot?'"

"I'll play the sodbuster. 'I' faith, if he be not rotten before he die—as we have many pocky corses now-a-days, that will scarce hold the laying in—he will last you some eight year or nine year: a tanner will last you nine year.'"

"*Your memory seems as muscular as ever, Mr. Emerson.*"

"*On that little word* seems *reality teeters. But yes, Mr. Whitman, this is one of my good days.*"

Hammond has passed on to another stone.

"*By God, Walt, I'll speak to the fellow!*"

"*It won't do for him to find* me *here.*"

"*Hide behind the obelisk. How Henry loathed that vain bulk of upstart masonry!*"

As Walt vanishes into the darkness, I approach Hammond, who has again dropped to his knees. When a dry twig snaps underneath my boot, he looks up and sees me standing over him.

"Why, Mr. Emerson! What brings you to Sleepy Hollow at this hour?"

"A nocturnal perambulation, Mr. Hammond, to walk off my dinner, to dispel the fumes of melancholy, to shake off muzzy-headedness. And what, if I may ask, are you doing with that tin funnel?"

He stands and eyes me sheepishly, as though discovered at some shameful practice.

"Well, Mr. Hammond?"

"Mr. Emerson, I've been out of my mind ever since last Tuesday, when I dug the grave of Widow Richardson here." He lifts the unshuttered lamp so that its yellow light falls on a newly chiseled inscription: MRS. CARY RICHARDSON, BELOVED WIFE OF MR. EDWARD RICHARDSON, ESQ., 1847–1879. "Did you know the lady?"

"She was married to the chief clerk of the county."

"I dug her husband's grave two summers back, during the diphtheria epidemic."

"And why, Mr. Hammond, are you kneeling at her grave, holding an ear trumpet?"

"After reading Poe's tale 'The Premature Burial,' I can't shake the thought from my head that some poor devil is lying in the coffin, screaming to be let out."

Briefly, the dead hear thuds of earth shoveled on their coffin lids before eternity packs their ears with cotton batting. But what if one of their number jolts into consciousness after the last mourner has departed? It is the scream of a boxed-up, terror-stricken human mole inside the little house that Hammond strains to hear.

"There's something in what you say. I heard that Charles Dickens ordered one of the new German coffins, equipped with a ventilator pipe, speaking tube, and a bell to give the alarm should he have a rude awakening. Poe, Chopin, even George Washington suffered from taphophobia, the fear of being buried alive."

"I don't know that anyone would much care for it."

"I am speaking of an irrational fear, Mr. Hammond. I feel its chill like a creeping damp."

My Cat Jeoffry . . . For he can swim for life. / For he can creep.

"You're shivering, Mr. Emerson! An October night can be cold and drear in the hollow."

The dampness smells like a piece of Walden Pond ice harvested by the Tudor Company's men from Boston, and of pine trees, their roots clawing the nearby banks of the Sudbury.

"Night is no time for a man of your years to be out of doors."

"Mr. Hammond, I would be free."

He shines his light onto a path that leads to a brick outbuilding whose casement window appears glazed with copper. "Let's go sit by the stove. I'll make us tea. What do you say? Shall we get into the warm and rest our bones?"

As we walk toward the cottage, the lantern light falls onto an ancient gravestone worn thin by time and rain, like a sliver of soap on a washhouse sink. The inscription is barely legible. I think the maggots eat our last words. Not content with our hearts, our livers, and lights, they crave the mind's integers. Death leaves us tongueless bells. I am walking in Walt's "mystical moist night air," but the sky framed by serried pines is empty of stars, as if their embers were extinguished in sympathy for the dead settled underneath them, embalmed in darkness.

Hammond bids me sit in the small room's only chair as he throws a scuttle of coal in the Hunt stove squatting on the flagstones. He puts the teapot on to boil and leans against the wall next to the window.

I'd put his age at forty or forty-five. His face is gaunt, like Lidian's; his skin tends to gray. His eyes betray a weariness beyond the common, affirmed by a sagging body that would resemble a partially emptied feed sack were he not so lean. He has the look of a man who used to eat and drink his fill and more but has lost flesh to illness or privation.

"Your brother-in-law stopped at Bush this evening to deliver our groceries."

"I hope you made sure that everything is in order."

Perplexed by his caution, I ask him to elaborate.

"Lyman Bierce is untrustworthy."

I sense that a story is about to be told and hope the tea will be ready before Hammond begins. I didn't realize how cold it is tonight until I stepped into the Sahara of the overheated room. There are a cot, a washbowl on a scarred maple dresser, and a map of the necropolis of which Hammond is lord and master. A row of handbells glints over the cot, each attached to a wirepull and topped by a black-edged card bearing a name inked in a fine hand. Following my gaze, Hammond explains that he prevailed upon the families of six of the recently departed to install bellpulls and ventilator pipes in their loved ones' coffins.

"If a bell should ring, I hurry to the grave and pump air into the coffin."

Demonstrating a pleated bellows, he assures me of its efficacy.

"I've heard said that, in foreign parts, undertakers sometimes pump smoke into a corpse's fundament before committing it to the ground, a practice that has occasionally worked miracles on the deceased."

This unsavory fact, no doubt of interest to the trade, is not, I confess, to me. I would report it to Poe, but having already arrived there, he is no longer curious about the afterlife.

Taking aim at me, Hammond squeezes his bellows. My thin hair riffles in the noxious breeze, and I feel my stomach turn.

We drink our tea in a silence disturbed by the clink of spoons against the cups, the soft combustion in the cast-iron stove, and—clamorous in my innermost ear—the peremptory ringing of the bells, as Poe heard and transcribed them.

> In the silence of the night,
> How we shiver with affright
> At the melancholy menace of their tone!
> For every sound that floats
> From the rust within their throats
> Is a groan.

Were a bell to sound in Hammond's graveyard cottage, I'd swoon away.

I turn my head from the annunciator and the repellent bellows and read the spines of a row of books leaning on a shelf above the desk where, I suppose, Hammond keeps accounts for the oblivious.

Moby-Dick, The House of the Seven Gables, Rough-ing It, Bleak House, A Christmas Carol, J. S. Le Fanu's *Ghost Stories and Tales of Mystery, Little Women, Knick-erbocker's History of New York, Poe's Tales, The Embalm-ing of President Lincoln,* by Charles Brown and Harry Cattell, as well as bound issues of *News from the Spirit World,* edited by Mrs. Adeline Buffum of Chicago. I'm gratified to see my own book *The Conduct of Life* among them, until I find that none of its pages has been cut.

Sitting on his cot, Hammond begins his tale.

"In '72, I went into business with Bierce, who was engaged to marry my youngest sister, Rose. Lyman seemed, in every respect, a good match for her. He was attentive, quick to do us all manner of little ser-vices, intelligent, keen, and likable. So when he pro-posed that we acquire the mortgage on a stationer's in Boston's Tremont Street, I agreed. As he was soon to be married to Rose, he convinced me—who was unmarried and likely to remain so after suffering a grievous wound at Shiloh—to put up the money for the venture. He'd see to ordering stock, maintaining the inventory, and doing the books while I served the customers. You might say, Mr. Emerson, that I was a first-class sucker, such as P. T. Barnum loves. And you'd be right."

Put-upon Mr. Hammond need not say another word for me to foresee the outcome of so naïve an arrangement. It's a story often told and almost laughable in its banality. So George's proved to be. Bierce played fast and loose with the creditors, and in a year and a month, Bierce & Hammond, Stationers, closed. George lost his money, Rose her bloom. By that time, the panic of 1873 had shuttered eighteen thousand businesses and banks. Any hope of a legal action brought against the embezzler disappeared in the universal rout. Wild speculation in railroads, ports, and factories during the boom years following the Civil War, the abandonment of silver specie in favor of gold, Europe's nerves rattled by the Franco-Prussian War, and the creation of a unified Germany—these and a myriad of other tangled influences combined to produce a depression that has yet to end. What was Lyman Bierce's finagling compared to the boondoggles of Jim Fisk and James Gould? The country was overrun by defalcators, defaulters, and debtors.

"Was there nothing you could do?"

"I could have killed him, and nearly did. The day he showed his face in Concord to move Rose and their child into his mother's house, I loaded my army Colt and marched over there to shoot the bastard through his coal black heart. Rose crumpled to the floor, threw her arms around my legs, and carried on while Bierce sat calmly on his mother's horsehair sofa with little Rose of Sharon on his lap. Then I did a shameful thing, Mr. Emerson, which I'll be sorry for as long as I live. In my fury and frustration, I put a bullet through his mother's dog. I'll tell you this, Mr. Emerson: If Lyman Bierce was nailed up in his coffin and his bell began to ring, I'd stick a rag in the ventilator! By God, I'd throw a stick of dynamite down the pipe!"

As my mind grows increasingly scrumbled, I think there is more truth in Poe's tales than in my philosophy.

"George, my friend, the world is as cold and damp as Fortunato's tomb."

"Mr. Emerson, I don't believe that to be the case, and I should know."

"I sometimes think my heart has been salted and put up in a stone jar against an endless winter."

"The world has shown me little warmth. Still, I don't complain, not as a rule. I'm better off than those out there."

Hammond jerks his chin toward the sad array of graves.

"Then you don't believe they're in a better place, or will be when the dead are awakened by the last trump?"

"I reserve judgment."

"Very wise of you, George. Did you know Henry Thoreau?"

"I met him years ago at Mill-dam. We argued over the best bait for catching pickerel. He had strong opinions."

"That he did. Did you ever hear him speak at the Concord Lyceum?"

"Can't say that I did."

"You missed a treat, not having heard Henry speak on subjects more controversial than fish bait. He has a sharp wit and no hesitation about using it on dunderheads. Mostly, however, he heaps scorn on our sacred institutions and our equally hallowed passion for acquisition at all costs. He likes to say, each man is, in miniature, a nation-state exercising its perceived manifest destiny and that nothing in heaven or on earth can stand in the way of it."

I realize that I've been speaking of Henry in the present tense, but Bierce took no notice.

"The last time we spoke was in Boston, by way of business. He was making the rounds of the stationery shops to demonstrate his improved plumbago pencil."

"Thoreau's Superior Ruler pencil."

"The same. The Germans may have had a better pencil than that manufactured by John Thoreau's company, but it was dear. I sold hundreds of the Superior Ruler during the thirteen months I had my shop."

Superior Ruler. Did Henry name it so to mock the Almighty tyrant or merely to promote his pencil's excellence?

Hammond has taken one of them from his drawer. He holds it up so that I can admire it.

Henry was an able mechanic. His grasp of

machinery gave his writing a practical aspect compatible with the Yankee temperament. My Jovian musings must seem a scant consolation to people who grapple with the facts of an onerous life, though none is likely to read them. I wrote, "Every spirit builds itself a house." In *Walden*, Henry left instructions on how to build one with wood, stone, and a keg of nails.

Of a sudden, I take it into my head to visit the pond and the site of Henry's cabin, which he abandoned in 1847—his experiment in living having reached a natural end.

"Mr. Hammond, what do you say to a walk in Walden Woods? I mean this very night to contemplate the ruin of my old friend's cabin."

I could have proposed that we scale Fairhaven Cliffs blindfolded and produced the same reaction in my host.

"Mr. Emerson, is that wise?"

Such folly entertained by the Sage of Concord is hardly to be believed now that night is pressing against the windowpanes, wanting to get in.

"The wisest thought I've had all day."

"You're not a young man, sir."

"I'll pretend to be otherwise, like a youthful actor who has donned the 'borrowed likeness of shrunk death.' Mr. Hammond, will you come?"

He has been idly marking the back of a deed to a tiny portion of Sleepy Hollow. I think it is the deathwatch beetle that he draws, or else a scribble of no import. I think that the only real estate is that to which Death has title forever and a day.

"No, sir. I'm sorry. I must keep watch tonight, in case . . ."

"You attend the dead as resolutely as Askalaphos did the orchards of Hades, in case one of the withered fruits should suddenly blush."

"It's my duty."

"Tell me, George. If someone should knock on your door, asking for help, would you give it or send him on his way with a sandwich and a piece of advice typical of Polonius?"

"If someone would come knocking at this hour, I'd jump clean out of my skin."

"I believe I would, too."

Temporizing, he lifts a stove lid and peers inside the miniature inferno; he stirs the hard black anthracite with a poker; he coughs, wipes his face on his sleeve; he puts the lid back, opens the stove's cast-iron door with the poker, rattles the clinkers, and slams the door shut with the toe of his boot.

"What sort of trouble is this fellow in?"

"He's a runaway."

"From what?"

"Judgment."

"Of this world or the next?"

"Does it matter?

"There's no escape from the final sentencing."

"This world, then."

"Men do get off scot-free."

He is thinking of Bierce, I expect.

"That's so, George."

Distracted, he crumples the deed he scribbled on. I hope it is not my title to the narrow lot that he conveys to the stove.

Like a boy peering through a shop window, I press my face against the cold glass pane.

"When I was young and brazen, I wrote, 'What I must do is all that concerns me.' I was convinced that I possessed the intuition and intellect to resolve every moral issue no matter how ambiguous."

"And now?"

"In town, they call me 'a crackpot.' No use in denying it, Mr. Hammond."

"I wouldn't think of contradicting you, Mr. Emerson."

"Tell them, God made nothing without a crack, except Reason, which is always sound."

"There's scarcely a moon tonight; the woods and pond will be pitch-black. What can you do in the dark?"

I shall pray to the local deity, whose name is Henry David Thoreau.

"If you must go, take my lamp. You won't see the path otherwise, or the trees."

"The spirit of man is the candle of the Lord." Proverbs 20.

"Won't you stub your toe on the gravestones when making your rounds?"

"I've another lantern. And take this, too."

Night's watchman takes a shawl from a nail and wraps my frail shoulders.

"You'll catch your death if you're not careful."

"I shall be in good hands if I do. Keep well, Mr. Hammond."

"And you, Mr. Emerson."

I will tear myself away from the sublime attraction of the grave and speak to Henry.

I leave the reserved fellowship presided over by George Hammond and strike out for Walden Woods. Except for the luminous swath sheared by the lantern from night's sable bolt, darkness garments me. A thousand times I've walked these woods—by day and night—but never has Death felt so near. A distant bell shatters the glass dish in which my heart steeps, and I imagine the watchman of Sleepy Hollow hurrying from his isle of light and heat to raise Lazarus from a counterfeit oblivion.

"Walt! Walt Whitman, are you there?"

No, say the trees. No, say the stones underneath my feet, tombs for the small lives that have perished there. No, say the night birds, whose jarring cries sing no one to his rest. No, says the lamp that sputters and goes out with a smirk.

Walt may have gone to talk to Hawthorne, although I suspect the conversation will be one-sided. Nathaniel had little to say in life and will have less in death. He saved his voice for his books.

I recall the alternatives that John Bunyan gave his pilgrim Christian: "So the one took the way which is called Danger, which led him into a great wood; and the other took directly up the way to Destruction, which led him into a wide field, full of dark mountains, where he stumbled and fell, and rose no more." Neither way is desirable for one whose feet hurt.

I recall Launcelot's madness and flight into the woods in Thomas Malory's book: ". . . speak we of Sir Launcelot, that suffered and endured many sharp showers, which ever ran wild wood from place to place . . ."

I am an old man alone in the dark and frightened for his mind's sake. I'm a pilgrim soul whose shoes pinch. Even Edwin Dietz's improved kerosene lamp has failed me.

I remember Hawthorne's description of Young Goodman Brown, who went stealthily into the forest at night: He "caught hold of a tree for support, being ready to sink down on the ground, faint and overburdened with the heavy sickness of his heart." But why, of a sudden, have *I* lost heart? Do I fear for Faith, from whom Goodman grew estranged, after having seen her dance naked with the Devil's brides?

Queenie, are you playing hide-and-seek in the woods, pink ribbons tied in your hair?

I wish the coming winter would not strip me of every leaf. I wish I were again a young man for whom death had no more sting than that of a bumblebee. I do wish the black man had not knocked on my gate with his stick.

Waldo, you're an ass to be afraid! No enchantment lies upon these woods; no devils inhabit them like those that terrified John Winslow's tiny settlement or the Pilgrims huddled by their rock.

I'm an ass to have attempted the journey—at night and a league distant!

Henry can walk it in three-quarters of an hour.

Henry wears seven-league boots and knows every twist and turn, every stone and tree that admonish me to forget the quest, whose purpose now seems childish. I pull the shawl closer and shout in a fluster, "Henry! For the love of God!"

"Waldo, what brings you to my woods at this hour?"

"I wanted to see the pond once more before my body is rent by Death, the great macerator."

"Come ahead, then."

"The lantern ran dry. I can't see the nose on my face amid these gloomy trees!"

"You've entered Walden Woods."

"I feel like Hansel after the birds ate his crumbs."

"A furlong more and your boots will be wet."

I walk and soon arrive at the edge of the pond. It is like a bowl brimming with silver. I have never before seen the effect, whose cause I can't determine, for the moon tonight is not so much as a paring of luminosity. I take hold of an alder branch to steady myself because the scene is beautiful and my knees tremble.

Old man, you mistake your eyes. No silver light lies on the water and the rounding trees. You are deceived.

No matter. To believe your own thought—*that* is genius.

Out on the pond, Henry is paddling his canoe. I call to him, but he doesn't answer. He lays the paddle aside and allows the canoe to drift on the argent surface.

Listen! He's playing his cherrywood flute, which Louisa Alcott exalted in a poem that included, among stanzas in praise of Henry, whom she once held dear in the naïve manner of young girls, this:

> Above man's aims his nature rose:
>   The wisdom of a just content
>   Made one small spot a continent,
> And tuned to poetry Life's prose.

"Henry! Come ashore and talk to me!"

I sit on the trunk of an overturned maple and muse on the fate of a photographic negative exposed to an excess of Radiance. The silver burns and blackens. Is this what happened to Henry and Hawthorne and is happening to Whitman and me? Were we all so vain and foolish, to think that we could look at the sun? Like silver particles, my words are burning out. To be buried alive would be like this, and I wonder who will dig me up when the bell tolls leadenly for me.

But before that happens, I must decide what to do about James Stokes. What a time for Henry to keep aloof!

"Damn you, Thoreau, I require your wisdom! Put down the flute and paddle ashore."

Doing neither, he fades into the engulfing darkness. As the pond gives up its splendor and the trees their silvering, my thoughts grow dim and dimmer still, till I am as a man delivered into obscurity. Within and without, the light is quenched, the black pond bears no image, and the firmament is empty of gods. The thread by which I'm related to all else trembles like gossamer caught in a breeze. A blow would break and orphan me.

I think James Stokes may be the excess of light that will destroy me.

I think he may be the wind that rises that will set me adrift.

"Henry, I need you to clarify a thing or two!"

His voice rises, then abruptly falls among the

briars, the nettles, the tangled vines. I am left with its echo.

"I can clarify butter, but little else."

It is a voice itself composed of quills and bristles.

"Do you recall—the memory just now jumped into view, like a school of herring, their scales soldered to their flesh sparkling in sunlight—when, on the Concord River, you dipped your paddle into the day's fiery remains and we left history behind us? I was imparadised."

He does not answer.

Petulant, I throw the useless lantern into the water.

I leave the pond to Henry's ghost and hunt for the place in the woods where he built his cabin when youth sat bravely and lightly on him, as God does on the seminarian. I taste ashes on my tongue, and hear again the death knell rung for my brothers Edward and Charles, my dear first wife, Ellen, and my sweet son Wallie.

> Ashes, ashes,
> We all fall down.

What earthly use is philosophy or poetry if it can't make a man any less afraid of death? What good is a thought or a verse whose author is beggared by time and, by time, is turned into dust—a poetical conceit for corruption, which is itself a euphemism for rot?

I find the cairn of stones brought by pilgrims visiting the shrine of their wood god. After Henry left it for good, his hut was carted off to the Clark place, near the opening of the old Carlisle road, where it fell to ruin. Nothing remains of it except the brick chimney, hearthstone, and cellar, which becomes the grave of a house left to stand empty until walls and roof tumble in and are shrouded by dead leaves.

> House you were born in
> Friends of your spring-time,
> Old man and young maid,
> Day's toil and its guerdon—
> They are all vanishing,
> Fleeing to fables,
> Cannot be moored.

Can only be mourned.

"It is better to go to the house of mourning, than to go to the house of feasting: for that is the end of all men." Ecclesiastes.

Above my head, universes are being spun of silken threads; each star is a drop of rain glistering in the light shed by the moon arisen after a storm has gone. A man or a woman does not require infinite spaces. Though larger than Prince Hamlet's walnut shell, Thoreau's meager kingdom by the pond was sufficient for his mind to rove the farthest planets, the nearest nest of spiders, and the aphids on the gooseberries.

If a moment is a concentrated eternity, what are

the millions upon millions of moments that constitute our lives?

To live a single moment should be enough. To suffer more than a moment would be to be bound, like Ixion, to a perpetually turning wheel.

Carlyle's words come back to me (as they sometimes will even now, as a bulb will thrust up through an April snow): "The withered leaf is not dead or lost, there are Forces in and around it, though working in inverse order; else how could it rot?"

To and fro, we are driven by what we cannot see. We mistake an action for evidence of progress, forgetting that a reaction must retard it. Like the bedazzled gaze fixed on a mesmerist's watch, our attention turns from simplicity to excess, from romanticism to classicism, until we are asleep. How hard it is to stay awake! How hard to awaken!

I remember the afternoon Lidian and I feted Nathaniel and Sophia Hawthorne, who were, at the time, living in Salem, where Nathaniel was employed by the customs service. We played croquet on the lawn. He called it "Newton's game," since the mallet imparted to the wooden ball a force equal to that which struck it. "In an ideal world," I said, "the ball would roll on forever." "Ah, but it's matter that makes the game interesting!" countered Nathaniel, whose idealism had been coarsened by a year of shoveling manure, during the noble experiment in communal living at Brook Farm, which failed.

And, by the famous might that lurks / In reaction and recoil, do we go about our days and nights.

Why doesn't the universe inside us blaze with an effulgence equal to that of the glorious universe that impinges everywhere on us? What matter weighs increasingly on our inward stars until gravity, which opposes our transcendent thoughts, has its way with them?

We don't know, say the trees that shiver in their nakedness. Neither do we, say the stones that iconoclastic boys shatter stained-glass windows with. Nor we, say the night birds, whose fierce cries splinter the bones in my chest.

Henry knew the names of trees, plants, birds, animals, rocks, minerals, stars. He knew that to name is to enlarge our understanding of the universe and, by doing so, become a perfect natural man. By the language of things do we attain the summit of what is possible for our kind.

I won't be a burrowing thing, a rock, a tree, no matter that it is evergreen. I would not be one of the brightest stars named by Hipparchus. I would not even be the astronomical proof of the existence of God. I *would be a man* standing on the ground in his boots, even if they pinch. To be a proper man or woman is more difficult than is commonly supposed.

A sound assaults my ears. Dismayed, I mistake it for Gabriel's horn summoning me to stand in judgment before the throne for impiety. But it's only a

Fitchburg locomotive raising the alarm to scare live-stock from the tracks. Once, I sued the company after sparks from one of its locomotives set fire to my woods. I lost. I would have needed young Mr. Lincoln to win a case against the vested interests.

Henry hated the railroads. But he was no Luddite who attacked factories at the onset of the Industrial Revolution, except as words could be bent to his purpose. He wrote that "if some have the pleasure of riding on a rail, others have the misfortune to be ridden upon." When Sam Staples asked what he meant by throwing apples at a passing Baldwin locomotive, Henry replied that he was feeding the Minotaur in the hope that it would choke.

Like a monk telling his beads, I pronounce the names of apples growing in my orchard: Baldwin, Golden Russet, Gravenstein, Spitzenberg, Winesap, Jonathan, Hightop, Bellflower, Tolman Sweet, Dutch Codlin, Sopsavine . . . How very lovely are the names of things! Walt Whitman knows that better than anyone.

I leave the woods behind and follow the Fitchburg tracks that lead to Concord. I stop to rest at the fairgrounds set in the corner of the field where the rails come near the Sudbury River, whence Henry and John once sailed onto the Concord River and thence on the Merrimack when they were green and careless. I think I see the two brothers rowing once again the boat they built and named the *Musketaquid*.

"Henry! John Thoreau! Where are you boys off to?"

"To the White Mountains to see God."

"Let me go with you!"

Henry laughs. *"There's no room in the boat for three such giants as we!"* Then he and his brother take up once more "The Canadian Boat Song," as they did many times in life:

> *Row, brothers, row, the stream runs fast,*
> *The Rapids are near and the daylight's past!"*

"I want to see His face, which I have seen only in His handiwork!"

Later, say the trees. Soon, say the stones. It's almost time, say the birds.

The blue-and-green boat has passed beyond the bend. The brothers will see the Great Stone Face scowling eastward from Franconia Notch. Is God's face made of granite, too? Has He hardened His heart against us, or does He weep glaciers over His fractious children? Was the fire that burned Sodom and Gomorrah only an accident caused by His scalding tears?

Twice I heard Him call me. The first time I was at the seminary. When I ascended the pulpit at Boston's Second Church, then, too, I heard Him. But the theology was cold mutton. I could find no pulse or warmth in the corpus given me to teach. Far better that a man examine himself than listen to another man's sermons. The Original is scribbled over with a thousand years of exegeses. I am become a little man of little faith, and the firmament no longer shines. "Fled is that music," sang Keats, who "wast not born for death." But he died notwithstanding.

Asleep in my house is Christ, as He has come again—a footsore fugitive, a black man, who could not, finally, turn the other cheek. He is hiding from Calvary in my dead friend's old bed. I hope that when morning comes, He'll have gone.

I consider walking to Monument Square, at the center of Concord, but decide against it. At this hour, the talkative dead will be recounting the Civil War battles in which they died. I fear my somber mood will not withstand the weight of all their sorrows.

The weight of sorrow is real, and so it was for me when I fled to Italy in the hope of easing my grief for my dead first wife, Ellen. Even as the boat steamed through the Strait of Messina toward Palermo, passing between famous Scylla and Charybdis, I was weighed down by a portmanteau in which I'd packed, unwittingly, the portion of Ellen that remained to me—my memories of her. I carried it in Palermo's public gardens, on its streets and lanes shadowed by the city's four hundred churches, and in the Capuchin vaults, whose damp nitered walls are lined with skeletons clad in burial clothes reduced, by time, to rags.

At Messina, I lugged that invisible portmanteau up Etna's steep volcanic slopes, like a pilgrim on the moon. I was beyond consolation, even that promised in heaven. What did I care for a Christian or Muslim paradise when I had savored it in Concord, Massachusetts, with my bride? There is one birth, one baptism, and one first love. For many years, I've lived with Lidian, but never have I felt the strength of passion that I knew for my enchanting friend. First love left a splinter in my heart.

Ellen, my own sweet girl.

In Naples, like many another ambitious young person uncertain of a career, except that it must bring him admiration, which differs from common fame, I thought that I might become a painter. As I gazed at the handiwork of Raphael, Titian, Guido, and Correggio, at portrait heads of Cicero, Aristides, and Seneca carved from alabaster or marble, at monuments to Dianas and Apollos without end, enthusiasm jumped up in me like a fire that purges the world's impurities, leaving behind the element sought by alchemists. *Enthusiasm*, I reminded myself, derives from the Greek phrase meaning "the god within." But the call to paint was soon muffled, as it was to preach, for which I had been trained and approbated. Only moral philosophy, poetry, history, and, later, science could—in Milton's phrase—spur me "To scorn delights, and live laborious days." In Naples, amid bottomless granaries of the spirit, Ellen was with me. Unforsaken by her, I was led to discover my purpose, which has had naught to do with the

God of Abraham and the Calvinists or even Him of Emanuel Swedenborg. Nature hates monopolies and exceptions.

There is no God in heaven, neither God nor heaven, except as we will them into an existence apart from our own.

What is that faint rumbling? Can He have sent the Juggernaut to crush me for my impudence?

No, it's only the tiny Minotaur inside the labyrinth of my gut. Of all the complaints a man can suffer, the flux is the most ignoble.

♣

Who can look upon a river in a meditative hour and not be reminded of the flux of all things?

"You still have work to do in the world."

I turn from the Sudbury River to the bandstand, whence came the voice—dry and hoarse, as if Demosthenes had put gravel in his mouth, instead of pebbles, to teach himself to speak in a silvered tongue. The voice belongs to someone who would not blandish or speak honeyed words. It rasped with the authority of those who believe themselves in possession of the truth. I used to speak thus, before the hinge of my tongue began to rust. What truth can there be, and how may one tell it when words—like leaves—have been beaten to the ground by such a storm as blasted Lear on his godforsaken heath?

"Your bewilderment is that of a man who has thought himself into a corner of his own making."

I walk toward the night-engulfed bandstand.

"Do I know you, sir?"

"In life, we were acquainted. I was a guest in your house when I spoke out in Concord against America's original sin, which persists even to this late hour."

I strain to see the man, but not even his silhouette is visible amid the shadows' heavy drapes.

"I am acquainted with many, and some of them have stayed at Bush with Lidian and me."

"You wrote of me, 'The Saint, whose fate yet hangs in suspense, but whose martyrdom, if it shall be perfected, will make the gallows as glorious as the cross.'"

It's John Brown, then, who captured the federal arsenal at Harper's Ferry and waited for the blacks to rise. None did. Those who managed to hear of his righteous assault could no more have joined him in revolt than a goose that has its feet nailed to the floor while its liver grows fat.

"Your words would have given me courage, had I lost it. But I'll tell you this, Emerson, good man that you are: I mounted the little stage of the gallows with equanimity, confident of the justice of my cause."

I despise goodies and religionists who, like speculators, take shares in heaven, as though it were a corporation promising an excellent return on their investment. Are you one of them, John Brown? Was I deceived in you?

"Although I eulogized you in Concord, I'm no longer sure you did right. You and your sons killed many and would have slaughtered many more. Your uprising would have been Nat Turner's all over again, only a thousand times bloodier."

"Nat Turner was a martyr for his race."

"He and his fellow rebels butchered women and children—even babes in their cradles."

"He did no more than God to the firstborn sons of Egypt. And so would I have done!"

"You, John, are not He."

I've climbed the stairs of the bandstand and am face-to-face with Brown. Although the night is dark, and darker still underneath the raftered roof, his countenance is made visible by a sickly green glow, such as may be seen on dead men left to sleep the night on a battlefield.

Brown spits as a man would after dislodging a pip from between his teeth. *"If someone's house is on fire, do you try to fathom the intention of Providence or pick up a bucket?"*

"You're the same hell-raiser as of old, I think."

Curious whether Brown landed in heaven or in hell after he dropped from the gallows, I sniff the air around him for the scent of either almond blossoms or brimstone. Neither is evident to my proboscis. (Asclepius, save me from a head cold! Lidian will eat my gizzard if she should hear of my nocturnal rambles.)

"Melville called me the 'meteor of the war.'"

"So he did, John."

"Abe Lincoln called me 'insane.'"

Of this much I am certain: Abe Lincoln basks in paradise, if heaven be anything other than a metaphor. I met him in '62, when I went to Washington to lecture on old age, though I had not yet reached it. The man impressed me greatly.

"Do you see much of the Great Emancipator?"

His reply will settle the matter of Brown's eternal whereabouts. Much to my annoyance, however, he will not say.

"John, what do you want of me?"

"You have a guest tonight at Bush—or should I say, you're harboring a fugitive?"

"Have you seen Stokes?"

"I have, and I should like to see him get up into Canada, where a negro can be free. He can't be in America—not now that the Reconstruction era has come to an end."

In March 1877, the Party of Lincoln betrayed the freed negroes of the southern states, in return for the election of its man, Republican Rutherford B. Hayes, as president. Federal troops garrisoned in the former Confederacy, by the authority of the Enforcement Act, to protect the lives and civil rights of blacks were recalled. States' rights–crazed Democrats got their way, the federal occupation of the South was finished, and the negroes were left on their own to face the arrow by day and the terror by night. Once more, self-interest and lust for power prevailed. The Klan is in the saddle and rides mankind.

"Emerson, what do you intend to do with your fugitive?"

Brown's shadow grows enormous, filling the bandstand and spilling onto the splintery grass. His voice assumes an ominous tone, as though he might hack me to death with a sword, as he did slave catchers beside Pottawatomie Creek, in the massacre by that name.

"I don't know yet."

In that little word *yet* lies the possibility of heroism or disgrace. I remember Montaigne's urging: "To be something, to be himself, and always at one with himself, a man must act as he speaks, must know what course he ought to take, and must follow that course with vigor and persistence." I was green when I first read that exhortation. Now I'm a dry old stick.

"Will you hand Stokes over to the army, or will you do as brave Boston did in the case of Shadrach Minkins?"

Minkins was seized when a slave catcher spotted him waiting on tables at Taft's Cornhill Coffee House. Upholding the Fugitive Slave Act of 1850, Massachusetts chief justice Lemuel Shaw—Herman Melville's father-in-law—ordered the runaway returned to his lawful owner in Norfolk, Virginia. The Boston Vigilance Committee, founded by my Transcendentalist friend Theodore Parker, plucked him from the courthouse, as the angel had done

Daniel from the lion's den, and sent Minkins to Canada on the Underground Railroad.

"Boston was not brave, John; twenty black men, led by Lewis Hayden, the committee's only negro member, rescued Shadrach from the federal marshals come to collar him."

I had spoken against the act, risking no more grievous bodily harm than a bloody nose given by an agitated Copperhead. My outrage at Mr. Minkins's capture did as much to liberate him as a damp firecracker would do against the jailhouse door. It needed black men to free the slave, and black men must keep them so, for no one else will.

Disobedience had been easier when, as a callow twenty-nine-year-old ecclesiast, I defied Unitarian doctrine and my congregation at Boston's Second Church. My hour of decision hung on the meaning of Christ's injunction to His disciples at the Last Supper: "Take, eat: this is my body, which is broken for you: this do in remembrance of me." From my Boston pulpit, I argued that Christ did not intend to enjoin all the generations to follow Him to observe a memorial feast. Because of a point no weightier than a gnat, I renounced my ministry. I'd have honored the God within me had I used the pulpit to denounce slavery, then and there, instead of waiting twenty years for runaway Thomas Sims to be delivered up, by the state of Massachusetts, to his former bondage in Savannah. At long last, I came out against the South's "peculiar" institution. If ever there was a word that scabbed over a wound, it is that! (Mark Twain would call it "beating the Devil around a stump.") To enjoy the taste of castor oil is peculiar; to own another human being and enjoy his pain is not. I was in no danger of martyrdom unless I were to be foolhardy enough to deliver an abolitionist lecture in Bloody Kansas, where a damned Yankee could be scalped.

Boston's abolitionists could not save runaway Anthony Burns when one hundred federal soldiers marched him from Boston Court House onto a south-bound ship that would deliver him once more into bondage and—should Colonel Suttle wish it—unto death by beating, hanging, tarring, or being flung into a vat of boiling sugarcane. Church bells tolled forlornly for Mr. Burns, while the citizens of Beacon Hill hung their heads in prayer and shame a moment, before going about their business. Only three Bosto-nians had the grit to interfere with the enforcement of a dirty law—Bronson Alcott, at whom the world has often sneered; Theodore Parker, Christ Militant of New England; and Thomas Wentworth Higgin-son, one of the Secret Six dedicated to John Brown and his righteous mission and, as I have heard men-tioned, confidant of the poet Emily Dickinson.

I study Brown's fierce eyes, his stern, craggy face framed by an ample gray beard. The Almighty would have such a countenance. Henry and John Thoreau could have saved themselves the trip to New

Hampshire had they stopped at the fairgrounds and looked upon the granite face of "Old" Brown.

"Anymore, John Brown, I lack all conviction."

"Waldo, you must act as if you were convinced, absolutely, of the truth—"

"As I see it."

"Or risk not acting at all—a renunciation of responsibility as culpable and damnable as Herod's when he washed his hands of the Lord."

"As to that, John, I'll answer as Krishna did Arjuna: 'It is necessary to act, undoubtedly, but to act as if one acted not.'"

I flinch as Brown comes toward me, the headland of his dark brow a thing to marvel at and fear.

"Have you taken up Orientalism?"

"If you don't care for the Bhagavad Gita, *I'll quote from* Les Misérables: *'To think is to act.'"*

"Horseshit! Will you think a homeless child into a warm bed and fill his empty belly with a thought? Will you think a drowning man onto shore, or will you throw him the life buoy at your feet?"

I pretend to a courage I don't have. *"Brown, you're too glib!"*

"And you have lost your backbone!"

His rebuke is a peal of thunder that must wake all Concord from its sleep, like the last trump. I shudder as it slowly fades toward the place where human noise is silenced. I sigh and sit wearily on a rustic bench.

"What would you have me do, John?"

"Save Stokes from the firing squad."

"And if he's not the good man we want to believe he is, because he is a black one?"

"That's God's business, not ours. Would you let him be taken and put to death because he might *be guilty? We're all guilty, Waldo, in God's eyes, if not in man's."*

"And should it happen to be that there is no God, except the divinity that resides in each of us?"

"Then we've kept faith with the best of ourselves."

I fall silent like one who has been roundly put in his place. I search my mind for a story to hoist me up again. What have we but stories that are, in Swedenborg's words, analogies and correspondences—emblems pinned to the real world beyond our weak eyes and meager reach?

"In Florida, where, in my twenties, I went to recover my health, I met Achille Murat, a nephew of Napoléon and a son of one of the emperor's marshals. Achille—he called himself 'Prince Murat'—had been banished from Europe after Waterloo, though he detested his uncle and, as a child, had once called him 'a wicked, wicked villain' to his face. He was charming, intelligent, congenial, and generous. He invited me to stay at his plantation in St. Augustine. He was writing a history of the United States. He was a good man, though he owned slaves and had a child by one. Should I have hated him?"

"If a man declares ownership of another man or woman, he deserves to be despised."

"As were you, John Brown."

"*As was I for having dared to free the four millions from their chains!*"

"*You failed.*"

His great voice thunders like a river's cracking ice. "*I did not fail!*"

"*Moral suasion might have taught the slaveholders charity.*"

"*Moral suasion be damned! Listen to your daemon, Emerson.*"

The eerie light on his face flickers out, and Brown is gone, at least from view. I hope never to see him again in this life or in the next. (Hell, I think, is a place of endless thought.)

Of a sudden, I feel a wind on my face. It carries the musty smell of libraries packed with old books or of the closets of old men. I think it is the odor of the past. I regard it with curiosity, like an antiquarian delicately sniffing the air for the scent of ancient artifacts. My nose, being of uncommon size, is a gross organ and perhaps not so keen as the connoisseur's that can detect dust laid down at the time of Washington and Lafayette or that which, lighted by the sun at his casement window, dazzled the eyes of Vermeer as it danced behind a luminous girl wearing a pearl in her ear.

Extravagantly fanciful?

How else can we who are mired in time and place escape them except by metaphor and hyperbole?

I close my eyes, longing to be abed and prey only

to a dreaming sleeper's commonplace terrors. Dickens gave Ebenezer Scrooge three ghosts to confront, but this day Providence has treated me to a veritable uprising of dead men. I do not think it is for my reformation that they come.

Not that I've done much harm in my life, which has been long and seems even now intent on squeezing a few more rancid lumps from time. I have been like the lucubrating snail, whose shiny tracks we sometimes see on philodendron leaves and which, night after night, persists in making its laborious trek, for a reason known only to snails (and Henry T., perhaps, whose eyes are gimlet sharp). One day they'll say of me, "He battered his brains against the bricks of books, the walls of stale custom, and the thick skulls of his contemporaries. For his efforts, we praise him, though they proved futile. For his indulgence of our folly, his cat Jeoffry licked his hands."

Arriving on a wind whose origin is July 4, 1837, I hear the town choir sing the "Concord Hymn" to the tune of "Old Hundredth," borrowed from the Genevan Psalter. The poem made me famous, as public verses can sometimes do, but the subtle lines that I've composed—elusive and reminiscent of the Persian—remain unknown by the *demos,* whom Whitman loves down to the odor of their armpits.

There is nothing of me in the "Concord Hymn." I was not among the embattled farmers facing the redcoats in our War of Independence's first skirmish, though my grandfather William heard the shot heard round the world—safely, gods be praised!—from a window of his house not far from old North Bridge. I was not at Bunker Hill, or Antietam, or bloody Shiloh, or in the Wilderness, nor did I witness "the fall of the Alamo, / Not one escaped to tell the fall of Alamo, / The hundred and fifty are dumb yet at Alamo," as rhapsodized by Walt Whitman. I was not even in Concord when the members of the town choir, Henry Thoreau among them, sang my hymn on Independence Day.

Nothing of me is in the "Concord Hymn," which I wrote at the urging of the Monument Committee. The man I am now exhales the sour breath of old age. I sing of conclusion; my new hymn is aptly named "Terminus":

> It is time to be old,
> To take in sail:—
> The god of bounds,
> Who sets to seas a shore,
> Came to me in his fatal rounds,
> And said: "No more!"

No more, say the trees in which sap has ceased to flow. No more, say the stones buried in the grave of time. No more, say the night birds who fall from the sky.

"'Quoth the Raven "Nevermore."'"

"Henry Thoreau, go spread your manure on someone else's field!"

In my orchard, which Henry and I tended many years past, pears ripen to perfection even if only in the mind. *Duchesse d'Angouleme, Saint Ghislain, Fulton, Dunmore,* and *Dix*—the words remain, though the trees perished from blight or neglect—time's sly pilfering. I say the words, and my mouth floods with the taste of pear.

On the dark road home, I fear meeting Margaret Fuller as she looked to those on the sea-swept beach when the brig *Elizabeth* missed Navesink Light and foundered off Fire Island, "in her white night-dress, with her hair fallen loose upon her shoulders."

The Carrara marble on board would not adorn the palaces of the nation's nouveau riche or our public concourses. After staving in the hull, it served Margaret as a cenotaph, heaped in careless remembrance on the ocean floor. "Keep your old-world stone," the gale winds might have shrieked. "Our native granite is sufficient for a democratic people to build monuments to commerce and to the heroic mythology of their birth." As the *Elizabeth* was breaking up on the bar, Fire Island's wreck pickers were going about their ghoulish business. They were no worse than Billy Spicer, who plunders apples and mince pies.

When bellies grumble, high-mindedness is forgotten. I forgive Billy Spicer, as well as scavengers who fatten on the beaches of wrecked hopes. The flight of the moth is preordained, as is the path trodden by the ant. Those who go their own way go mad.

Is the life of a slaver, a breaker, a man paid to hunt fugitives also preordained?

Damn words—their barb has hooked my lip!

I no longer remember how to be human. I remember only how to be afraid.

Many times I have beaten back the memory of a summer's day when I was eight and my father dropped me from the wharf into the sea to teach me how to swim. The baptism left me in mortal terror of a watery death! Margaret, how I miss you! In time, I was reconciled to the death of my son, my brothers, and my first wife, but not to yours, although I'd scream were you to step out from a break in the hedges and accost me! Were my imagination of the morbid kind, I might pen a tale as horrific as any by Poe or Le Fanu. It tends, however, toward the sublime rather than nature's grosser part.

In a darkness engulfing as a monk's cassock, I trip on an elm branch felled by Monday's storm, which rattled Concord's windows and tore shingles from the roofs. Every appearance in nature corresponds to a state of mind. For this reason, I prefer *tormenta*, the Spanish word for tempest. The wind and rain pained the townspeople, their houses, and the earth itself, which, Henry maintains, is aware of our kind's presence, as a bison is a tick or Leviathan a whaleman's harpoon. I pick up the stick at my feet and lean on it like a pilgrim on his staff.

"Waldo, how feeble you've become! I hardly recognize you."

Just as I feared, Margaret accosts me. In appearance, she is what you would expect of someone who drowned three decades past, save that she speaks. Ridiculously, I find myself at pains to account for my unprepossessing self. I plead the accidental encounter, the darkness, a stiffness of the joints that makes my gait other than she remembers from our fervent youthful days in Concord, before she went to Florence.

Margaret! What seedsman sowed your genius in our hard New England soil? It was New England's good fortune, and mine, that you took root here, as it was also when it smiled on the auspiciously named horticulturist Robert Fortune, who brought China's glorious natives—the rhododendron, forsythia, and verbena—to blaze in our common earth.

She laughs delightfully. *"Digressive, as always, Mr. Emerson."*

"You read my mind."

"I know it all too well."

"Margaret, you were an exotic in our rough-and-tumble democracy, one who could not truly flourish until you went to live among the cultured Florentines."

For us, her friends, she was a finished creation. We could not have foreseen that she would touch the sublime during the siege of Rome, when she bandaged soldiers' wounds wet with republican blood shed by the army of Louis Napoléon. Nor could we have imagined that she would break the bread of her body with a patriot from one of Italy's noble houses and bear him a son. It's no shame on her to have been eager to part with a virginity that hampered her passionate nature. It was a needle's eye that she had need to thread to enrich the embroidery of her soul.

"To think you died just sixty rods from your Ithaca! What a hero's welcome you and your Ossoli missed! We would have drawn your carriage through the streets of Concord."

"Fate is cruel, Waldo, and God many times unkind."

"God the amnesiac, who has forgotten us all."

She mistook my self-pitying observation for a vestige of an inextinguishable grief.

"I can but accept the pages as they turn."

"I sent Thoreau to search the beach for your body, but it was never found."

By a shrug of an alabaster shoulder, Margaret gives me to understand that her corpse is of no concern.

The walking stick bites my hand.

"In truth, it was your manuscript that I hoped Henry would find on the beach. I'd have given much to have

your history of Italy's 1848 revolution. Had you lived, you might have been our Carlyle!"

She turns her gaze on me. Had it shone through the lens of Navesink lighthouse, where the Atlantic shoulders its way into Lower New York Bay, the *Elizabeth* would have safely reached her berth on the Hudson. And Margaret, my friend, would have come ashore and claimed her portion of the enlarging American mind. How she does look at me! I feel like the ecstatic mast of a sea-lashed ship in the midst of a galvanic storm. Unless . . .

I rub my hand over my jaw.

"I don't have another of those odious carbuncles, do I?"

"You look as handsome as ever, Waldo dear, and the set of your jaw is as brave."

How brave *she* was to have gone abroad not as Americans grandly do to view the frescoes and the ruins! She was taken up by Carlyle and George Sand and heard Sand's lover Chopin play in her Paris apartments. Her letters brimmed with passion and praise for France and Florence.

"'Et quae tanta fuit Romam tibi causa videndi?'" I ask her, quoting Virgil. What was the urgent business that took you to Rome?

"Libertas."

The French crushed the infant Roman Republic and restored the House of Savoy and the Pope to their former glory. General Garibaldi and his four thousand legionnaires withdrew to the Apennines, Margaret and Ossoli to Florence, where she wrote a history of the revolution. In May of 1850, having grown weary of the Old World and hankering for the New, she, the marquis, and their two-year-old son, Nino, sailed from Livorno aboard a merchantman brig. They came within sixty rods of the shore—nine hundred paces—fewer than Bush is from the post office and the shops! A convulsion of wind and waves flung them all into the sea, careless of her brilliance and poetry, while the Sage of Concord pondered fate on Nagog Hill.

I take my hat off to her.

"Margaret, regardless of its brevity, you lived a splendid life!"

Would that you, too, could have walked on water!

"Your life, Waldo, which is tapering toward its end, is still being measured."

"Like a corpse for its coffin."

"To speak without adornment, yes."

"Then you're aware of my dilemma."

"Just now I overheard one of your harshest critics."

"Brown thinks I play at philosophy, when I should act."

"The earth is drenched in blood spilled by those who act. I saw as much in Rome. But yes, those who shed it were magnificent!"

I take the devil's part. *"They acted blindly."*

"Who of you isn't being spun around in a game of blindman's buff?"

I shout to my sleeping village neighbors, "Is there no one who can tell me what I must do?"

Margaret laughs, since she has passed the need to endure, to think, to act, even to be. Although her body was never found, her life is aptly summarized on a stone in Mount Auburn Cemetery:

> BY BIRTH A CHILD OF NEW ENGLAND
> BY ADOPTION A CITIZEN OF ROME
> BY GENIUS BELONGING TO THE WORLD

"Is there anything you would like to know before I go?"

"Was Bishop Ussher correct, after all, when, in his Annals, *he declared that creation commenced at the beginning of the night that preceded the twenty-third of October in the year 4004 B.C.? Or does Charles Darwin grasp the truth of the matter?"*

"Tsk, tsk! What a foolish mortal you can be, for a sage!"

"I grant you that."

"Good-bye, Waldo."

"Must you go? Wait, at least, until the sun comes up. It'll warm our ancient bones."

"Each night I walk the beach in the hope that the sea will give up its dead and I shall be reunited with my son and my beloved Giovanni."

I twiddle my stick; I scratch runes in the dirt

road with it; I fling it into the hedges for the hedgehogs to gnaw.

"Remind me, Margaret, were we ever in love?"

In her eyes, which are lighted from within, as if
they had absorbed the flames of the bonfires set by
the wreck pickers on Fire Island, I see pity, sadness,
tenderness, and spite.

"Is love so important, Waldo?"

"I think it must be, for me to ask."

*"Then you don't remember having told me that love is
only phenomenal, a contrivance of nature?"*

*"If I'm to eat my words at this late hour in my history,
I'll go on tour with Barnum as the world's fattest-headed
man, if I don't die first of dyspepsia."*

"Arrivederci, fratello."

Margaret goes, leaving me to carry on in an
unfinished play in which I've been given the leading
role against my will and whose final pages I have not
read.

By the bell tolling solemnly from the spire of First
Parish Meeting House, the time is a quarter past,
although I can't tell to what hour night has advanced.
Has October 21 been almost drained from the barrel,
or has a new day already been tapped?

Or has the hour of my Gethsemane come round
at last?

Even now, Emerson, your arrogance is staggering!

I search the night sky for a sign of God's displea-
sure. I could almost pray for Him to send a meteor to

knock out my brains or a fire bolt to incinerate me. But the sky is uninterested in the fate of Ralph Waldo Emerson; not even the stars, which are uncommonly faint tonight, shed their influence, malign or otherwise, on me. I may as well be a blind mole, so distant am I from the Radiance, or an ancient tortoise of Galápagos, so deaf am I to universal harmony. Tonight the world seems a scaffold erected for divine vengeance. From my pocket, I take my old compass, which I've always thought of as evidence of the god of nature and of universal law in its unerring and incorruptible virtue, but the needle swings wildly.

A scream from the poorhouse across Mill Brook shivers night's darkened panes; Nancy Barron is once again beset by terrors known only to the mad. I tell myself, What's this Hecuba to me? I would shake my head to be rid of her shrill declamation, but I'm reminded that Solomon gave heed even to the plaintiff gnat. If nothing else, I must lend an ear to the woebegone. God knows, I've had much to do with lunatics in my life.

Now who is *this* hurrying toward me? I won't stand another visitation, even if it is for my benefit. I tremble in expectation and grope for the shawl to conceal myself, but it is gone from my shoulders—snagged, perhaps, by a branch as I blundered through the woods. What will I say to Mr. Hammond tomorrow after having lost both his lamp and shawl? He will think me a senile old man—and I am. You are,

Emerson! Tomorrow may find me utterly at a loss for words. I'll attempt to convey my apologies, using the alphabet of the Chinese or, like an illiterate, sketch them in the dirt with the pointed stick. Blast me for a fool! I threw the stick away and am too weak to wrest it from the sharp teeth of the hedgehogs. I'll take Hammond an offering of watermelon pickle— or a mince pie, if Billy Spicer has not raided the larder during my ramble.

It's too late to dodge or hide. The man bearing down on me swings his hurricane lamp aloft to get a look at my face. His is equally illuminated by it. We greet each other with mutual surprise.

"Mr. Emerson!"

"Dr. Bartlett!" Certainty dissolves after the day's strange events. "You *are* he, are you not?"

"Who else?" To confirm his identity, he produces, from beneath his hat, an uncommonly large head, bald as a pear. "Mr. Emerson, what're you doing out of doors at this hour? With your lungs, it's a fool's errand!"

"We do not breathe well when infamy is in the air."

Raising his lamp, Bartlett gives my face a second look, then shakes his head gloomily at the possibility of another deathbed visit before the night is out or my commitment to the asylum where my brother Bulkeley urgently recited the multiplication tables in the hope of attaining the infinite.

"I've been on a pilgrimage. By the way, what is the hour?"

He consults his hunter watch; the lamp follows his rising arm. I smell kerosene.

"Eleven thirty."

"Strange, I thought it later. I could have sworn I heard the lark, herald of the morn."

He glances at me as if there were indeed a carbuncle on my face, needing to be lanced.

"Put this on, Waldo. Your coat is too thin for the night air."

He means to give me his, but I refuse it with a churlish gesture I immediately regret.

"Thank you kindly, Doctor, but I'm nearly home."

"A pilgrimage, you say?"

"I've been visiting a few old haunts."

"Couldn't they have waited till tomorrow?"

"The past is best viewed at night, when extraneous detail is erased."

He gives me a curious look suitable to his profession. Theologians are never curious, believing the universe is adequately explicated in the Bible, if one only cares to look, or else beyond the comprehension of mortals; in which case, curiosity is a waste of time that good churchmen can spend more profitably in writing sermons and hobnobbing with parishioners at church fetes.

"I'll look in on you tomorrow, Waldo. I'll give you something to settle your nerves."

"And what was your business in the world tonight, Doctor?"

"Old Miss Greenwald died."

"I know the lady. I assume you did your best by her."

"There was little I could do, except to make her easy. Her heart gave out."

"The heart almost never hesitates. It knows its mind."

He nearly bristles at what would sound to his professional ears like a criticism.

"She was eighty-eight!"

"When I see her, I'll tell her that you did your best."

"Waldo, you're raving." He holds the lamp near my face. "Your eyes have a strange cast in them tonight."

"As they should after what they've seen and heard—my ears, it was, that did the hearing. My eyes were preoccupied. I won't have you thinking I suffer from synesthesia! I leave the rare complaints to Lidian. There are many gnats in the air tonight. They come from the grass to speak with Solomon."

He offers me his arm. "Let me take you home."

"Don't trouble yourself, Dr. Bartlett. I'm only thirty yards, more or less, from the place where I lay me down to sleep."

In the pleated space between "more or less," the world can end. In it, I will say again the names of the pears I love. Bartlett, being the least exotic in my orchard, I'll save for last. Henry calls the graveyard "the bone orchard." What a gift for the vernacular he has!

"Waldo, is Lidian at home?"

I lie to spare myself further solicitude, which can be tiresome, except for that shown by a faithful dog, whose affection never cloys.

"She is."

"Get some rest. I'll be by tomorrow and dose you. I'll bleed you if I see no improvement."

"I thought your trade considered bleeding old-fashioned."

"It has its uses, regardless of what they say in Berlin."

"Good night, physic."

"Good night."

He offers me his hand. I give him mine, thinking he means to shake it. He presses his thumb to my wrist and, with his watch, takes my pulse by lantern light.

"You've had a hectic night, I think."

"Doctor, were you in church the day I resigned my pulpit?"

"You know I was raised a Methodist, and would've been no older than ten or eleven at the time."

To be again the fiery young man who brazenly bid his congregation farewell, declaring, among a number of well-put blasphemies, "I regard it as the irresistible effect of the Copernican astronomy to have made the theological scheme of redemption absolutely incredible." The truth is that I wanted religion to astonish me, as much as I wanted to startle the righteous out of their starch.

Bartlett turns and walks toward town as the beam from his lamp jumps nervously on the road before him. Of a sudden, a beast charges from a stand of pines and gnashes its teeth at the moving light. But it's only Finnegan's dog, Wolfe Tone, named for the Irish patriot and martyr.

> There was an old man named Michael Finnegan.
> He grew fat and then grew thin again.

Had it been a hellhound or the three-headed Cerberus, my heart would have given out like poor Miss Greenwald's.

Greenwald is a lovely word. Isn't it, Henry?

"Good night, Waldo, my friend."

His voice fades into the beech wood, like notes of a whippoorwill scattered by the wind.

I take a few halting steps toward my house. The wise man hesitates, to foil impulsiveness, that enemy of reason. I lean against the Alcotts' fence. Through the parlor window, I see Louisa at her writing desk. Oh, to feel once more the exultation that follows the fluent lines of ink, the veins and arteries of thought itself laid down on paper for the world to see and marvel at! To write a few lines of doggerel would please me now that I'm dogged by the bitch forgetfulness. Today she granted me a reprieve, and I knew again the joy of articulate speech and thought, though my own poem continues to be recalcitrant. But the joy is a counterfeit, and I will suffer all the more for it tomorrow, or the next day, or on a day next month when I look at Queenie's face and ask, "Who are you?"

Coleridge wrote, "*Quantum scimus sumus.*" We are what we know.

What will I be when I know nothing?

To confirm my mind's disarray, the First Church bell strikes thirteen and fear in my heart, withal, that sets me quaking. Mad with terror, I rush onto the Alcotts' porch and clap the front door, as if I would bring down the house.

"Waldo, you're trembling! Whatever's the matter? Come in and warm yourself. What possessed you to go outside without a hat and scarf?"

It appears that I lost the first after taking it off to Margaret in the road. I can't think what I did with the second article, which I remember having put around my neck before I went abroad.

"Is Mr. Stokes all right?"

"He's asleep in Margaret Fuller's bed."

I'm as wobbly as Humpty Dumpty before his great fall.

"Those who spend their days prating of philosophy end up sitting on their brains. This, Lu, is the true meaning of *pratfall*."

The look on her face is one that I have seen frequently on Queenie's.

"When does Lidian get back from Edith's?"

"Tomorrow, or the day after."

"And where is Ellen?"

"Wife Ellen lies in her grave, testing her belief in the sure and certain hope of the Resurrection. Daughter Ellen has gone to Boston to hear Jenny Lind sing."

"Sit down. Let me get you a glass of sherry."

"No sherry. I wonder, does Bronson keep something more fortifying in the house?"

She bites her lower lip in skepticism and then goes to the sideboard in the dining room. After a momentary chiming of bottles, as musical in their way as the six planets transcribed by Kepler in *Harmonices Mundi*, she returns with a bottle of Boodle's British gin. I suspect not even Walden Pond's water is so pure as this aromatic distillation of the grain.

"Thank you, dear girl."

I pour a full four fingers' worth of the juniper-scented elixir and drink it in one go.

"You're becoming a sot, Emerson. I'll report you to the Daughters of Temperance."

"Go back to Camden, damn you, Walt!"

Whitman is a Minotaur of a man, brazen, monstrous, and terrifying. Let him prowl the dank halls of the Labyrinth while I roam the stars till their machinery creaks for want of oil.

"I'll oil the works, if need be! Every last tooth and gear!"

"Ralph Waldo Emerson! You'll be sick." She takes the bottle away. "You're not used to ardent spirits."

"I've been entertaining them all day."

"How will I explain to Lidian if Sam Staples jails you as a public nuisance?"

"Each man is a public and a nuisance unto himself, Lu."

You were the best of them, Henry David Thoreau!

The gin has done its work. I feel atoms of tranquillity coursing through my veins. I lean my head on a tatted antimacassar and prepare to be pleasantly stupefied.

"You can't spend the night on my sofa, Waldo! If anyone should find you here in the morning, it would spell the ruination of your career as a moral philosopher." She is smiling agreeably.

"*R–U–I–N–A–S–H*. Damn it, Louisa May, how is it spelled?"

"Get up before you ruin the antimacassar."

"Antimacassar. What an ugly congeries of sounds! Ah, but there is no lovelier word than *pharaoh*. *P–H–A–R–O*, or is it *A*? Never mind. *Elephant* is also fine, as is . . . I can't tell its name, but I can tell its history. Strangers take it away. Oh, well, I'll remember tomorrow, or not. Giving the ear pleasure, as some words do, they ought to produce a wholesome effect on the soul. I shall write a letter to the archbishop of Boston, recommending that children be made to say them in lieu of the *Pater Noster*. For punishment, I'll suggest *antimacassar* to his Excellency. The rod will be spared, but the child not spoiled."

"You're not the least yourself tonight."

"Perhaps I'm *most* myself tonight."

"Waldo, I hardly seem to know you."

I would not have known you the day your father brought you home from Georgetown. Your face looked queer, thin, big-eyed. How sad we all were when they cut off all your hair, a yard and a half, and—in that marvelous expression—you "went into caps like a grandma." You were frightened of a Spaniard wearing black velvet who popped from the closets like a jack-in-the-box.

"There've been times, dear Louisa, when I wished I could be somebody else—anyone other than Ralph Waldo Emerson, whom posterity will remember as a scholar and a poet, and whose wife as a distant, chilly man. Shame on him!"

She eyes me strangely, a little fearfully, as anyone sane would a madman in the house. I sometimes think a common mind is desirable; an uncommon one is a rack on which its possessor is stretched near to breaking.

I wander idly about the room. Putting on my spectacles, I glance at a sheet of paper tracked with ink on Louisa's small desk.

"Are you writing more of Jack and Jill?"

"I'm writing to May's husband, Ernest. My sister is very ill, and I fear the worst, although his last letter from Paris gave me some reason to hope."

"I didn't know."

"You *did* know, Waldo. You forgot."

"I suppose I did. What's wrong with May?"

"A distemper of the brain."

"She's so very young and accomplished to . . ."

"Die?"

"Not to go on living."

"Death doesn't spare youth or talent and won't be circumvented by a circumlocution."

"And here I am—a useless, forgetful old fool of seventy-six! I'd gladly go in her stead."

"Few are given the opportunity."

"Not true, Louisa, though the opportunities present themselves in unexpected guises."

Bemused, I bite my finger.

"Let me see you home, Waldo."

"Not until we've conjugated Jack and Jill."

"Please, let me take you home."

My temper rises no higher or hotter than a squib. Ah, to feel the heat of indignation that once made overcoats and shawls superfluous! "Louisa May, I'm not so old that I can't cross the road."

I'm too old, however, to be seized by a "casting moment," like that granted me at Mount Auburn Cemetery when I realized that our animal life is an incorporation of nature, and nature an emanation of the one great truth. We are circles enclosed by circles, and in our turn, we enclose smaller ones. We are caught in a mesh of correspondences ranging from infinitesimal to infinite, which are one. I was pierced, there, as if by the tines of the fork that tunes the universe with the one inside us. Surrounded by the clapperless dead, in that still place where time is adjourned, I imbibed the liqueur of fire—the soul's noblest part, according to Heraclitus. Never again will I taste fire. From now until my light and music have fled, I will have to make do with warm milk.

"Waldo, I worry that you're alone in the house tonight."

"But I'm not. Mr. Stokes is there."

I start for the front door.

"Wait!" She throws her velvet cloak around me.

"Louisa, is it your wish to unman me entirely?"

"Nonsense! There's no one about at this time of night to see you."

"That's what you think. There's a mob of folks abroad in Concord tonight."

"What rubbish you've been talking! You're really not yourself. Are you feverish?" She lays the back of her hand on my forehead. "On the contrary, your brow is cold as ice."

It has not warmed since I pressed it to Mr. Hammond's window overlooking Sleepy Hollow's dead.

"Walden Pond's ice is universally admired for its purity. In Calcutta, maharajahs cool their sherbet with it, or so Mr. Tudor of Boston claims. Advertisements are weightier than the Gospels in our Gilded Age. Isn't it strange that many should be skeptical of the Almighty when they believe every word of Mr. Tudor, Mr. Fisk, and Mr. Barnum?"

Once again, Louisa attempts to foist her cloak on me. This time I concede—too weary to protest.

"Send Mr. Stokes to me at once if you should take sick."

"If you see my house burning, don't send for the fire brigade."

I leave in a colicky mood and am too peevish to admit that I was ungracious to Louisa. Gaining the opposite pavement, I turn and see her anxious face at the window. I wave—gaily, I hope—and go inside my house, which is cold and dark.

Stokes may have left without bothering to light a lamp or lay a fire. I, who scorned the old conventions of custom and belief, would forgive his rude departure, would, in fact, revel in it.

Or perhaps, in his exhaustion, Stokes slept through the night's arrival and is sleeping still.

Or might I have imagined him?

No, Lidian spoke to him in the kitchen before she left for the depot. And that scoundrel of a grocer did, as well. And I remember the bloody clouts Louisa put into the stove.

Mr. Emerson, how you dither! Soon you'll be as resolute as the igneous folk dug up at Pompeii, who are beyond all vagaries and questions. Twenty years ago, while excavating that ancient town, Giuseppe Fiorelli discovered Roman couples in their beds, surprised by the sudden fires of Vesuvius. Nothing remained of them—not even their unromantic bones. Only cavities were left in the hardened ash, which Fiorelli filled with plaster of Paris, as the rabbi of Prague had made golems out of clay. Some Pompeiians had perished in each other's arms, while others had been lying back-to-back, steadfast in anger or indifference, for nearly two millennia. If one night the Concord River should flood and entomb Queenie and me in mud, our neighbors will wonder if we had been estranged or merely bashful.

What a prig I've been! We had just set out on the road we vowed to walk together when I insisted on calling her Lidian, so that I could invoke, at my pleasure, the voluptuous measures of Anatolia. Lydia—the given name of a self-reliant spinster of Plymouth, Massachusetts, whose mind is fierce and hard as flint—was not sufficiently poetical for R. W. Emerson. And how I insulted her proud Yankee nature and intelligence when I began to call her

"Asia"! No wonder the flowers brought from her yard at Winslow House died in the mephitic atmosphere of Bush! It was a chilly life I brought you, Lydia Jackson, when we married in that house you loved and you renounced for one in Concord, which we shared with my mother and brothers. It was a cold man you took to wed and bed. While you charmed sweet airs from the piano, I played the ice harp to the cold fire of the stars.

My spirit has been wrung from the rag of my body. I'm prepared to let fate decide the outcome of this day's vexations. The pillars of portentous night are cracked; the roof is waiting to fall.

Too low in spirit to mount the stairs, I lie on the sofa. The hearth fire unmade, the room is dark, like the night waiting behind my lids. If I should not wake when the sun does or if it refuses to play its part tomorrow, sick of its endless diurnal round—what then, Waldo?

"O let me rise / As larks, harmoniously . . ."

As larks! How lovely is George Herbert's happy union! What a wedding of words! But what if tomorrow I should forget the songbird's name?

"So long as you remember its song."

"Watch over me tonight, Henry, il miglior fabbro. *Stave off oblivion awhile longer."*

I fall and then rise again into a world that is very much as I left it. Sitting up on the sofa, I recall a curious dream from the night just past.

I was in the Spedale dei Pazzi, an asylum I had visited during my stay in Palermo. In the dream, I wore a black seminarian's gown, which shrouded my sloping shoulders and emaciated frame, like a cloth thrown over a parrot's cage. On their knees, the poor mad folk were walking toward me across the flagstones. I found an aspergillum in my hand and sprinkled them with holy water. At each drop, they screamed, as the mandrake root is said to do when pulled up from the ground, the sound of which will kill anyone who hears it.

"Why do they scream?" I asked a porter.

"It is pleasing to God's ears, signore."

"Tell me, how did I get here?"

"You entered through one of Piranesi's dreams."

The seed of madness lies dormant in the Emerson stock. Bulkeley and Edward sojourned at the McLean Asylum, in Charlestown, Massachusetts, entranced by *les fleurs du mal* of their own making. Having succumbed to his mind's disease, Bulkeley is buried not far from Hawthorne, the melancholiac. Edward sleeps nearby, along with our brother Charles. Soon, I, too, will lie in Sleepy Hollow. Restless beneath a marker of rose quartz, I'll recite the conjugations of the verb *be* into George Hammond's ventilator. Lidian will join me in her own good time, since not even the Almighty can hurry her, who is stubborn in the way some are who appear sweetly obliging.

"Get up, slugabed, and shake your lazy bones!"

"Lidian, are you home?"

"It's Henry. It's going on nine o'clock. Mr. Stokes has been up since dawn."

Through the window, I see him kneeling in the yard; perchance he's pulling mandrakes. By his presence, I know that God or my ruthless destiny has not taken the bitter cup from me; on the contrary, I'm bidden to drink as deeply as I did last night of Edward Boodle's gin. I've been spared a chastening headache, if nothing else. Wriggle as I will like a worm on a hook, there's no escaping me.

In the kitchen, I find the stove has been lighted, and a loaf of bread is in the oven.

Stokes comes in, carrying an armful of wood.

"Good morning, Mr. Emerson."

"You've been industrious, Mr. Stokes, while I slept."

He stacks chopped wood in the corner. "I baked some bread for you and Mrs. Emerson."

He opens the oven's squalling door, pokes the loaf with a broom straw, and, satisfied of the bread's material condition, sets it on a stove lid to cool. If only our spiritual condition could be as easily assayed! Alas, not even a straw plucked from a Shaker broom can test the consistency of a conscience.

He busies himself fixing my breakfast. I guess

he means to wheedle a concession. But my mean-spirited cynicism is undermined when he announces, "I'll be on my way, Mr. Emerson. I didn't want to go until I thanked you. I got a good sleep, and I helped myself to a couple of eggs for my breakfast."

His dark brown eyes search my watery pale blue ones. What do you hope to convey by that gaze, Mr. Stokes? Your very presence in the room would seem to censure me.

He closes his mouth; his lips compress. Do you mean to pout, Mr. Stokes? He makes a face that may connote either friendliness or scorn. Who can tell what thoughts actuate a human heart or conduct the mind's music? Authors may claim to know, but it is only their own creations that they understand. Human character is as illegible as an inscription on a wafer-thin headstone belonging to one of Concord's ancient dead or on the plaster mask of a vanished Pompeiian.

I am something other than relieved, like a schoolboy who, having diligently prepared to sit an examination, feels both spared and let down when the proctor does not come. When Stokes goes, I may not have another chance to test the courage of my convictions. In a day or two, I'll have completely forgotten him and the uncertainty he brought into my hermitage.

"Sit, Mr. Stokes. The bread smells miraculous. Have some for your trouble—and don't be afraid to chew, since it isn't Christ's body I'm giving you to eat."

"Thank you, sir. I find I'm hungry again."

"Let's have some butter for the bread."

I fetch butter from the buttery, along with some cold meat and mustard, and two bottles of strong ale. I glimpse John Brown scowling at me. Madly, I stick out my tongue at him. Stokes takes no notice. I feel a sudden affection for him. Isn't it often so when a troublesome guest is ready to depart? We put a hand on his shoulder, smile warmly, and beg him to stay one more day. And now I find that I've done that very thing! What madness!

"I guess it'll be all right. Thank you, sir. Anyhow, it's better I leave when it's dark."

Immediately, I am beset by yesterday's doubts. Do I want to spend the few years left to me in prison for aiding and abetting a fugitive?

A cobweb overlooked by Lidian's broom trembles at the disembodied voice of John Brown: *"I'd blow up the universe twice over to save Mr. Stokes! I'd set the sea on fire!"*

I gather the dirty plates and take them to the sink. The crumbs call to mind the saleratus biscuits I ate beside the Tuolumne River, on the trail toward the Valley of the Yosemite.

"Brown, I'm sitting the horse I was given and will ride it to the end."

A steam locomotive shrills derisively. The ten o'clock train from Boston.

I fill the sink with water and put the things to soak.

"I saw one of your books on the table beside the bed."

"Did you read any of it, Mr. Stokes?"

"No."

"There's nothing in it worth your time."

"I like a good yarn. Did you ever read any of Bret Harte's tales?"

"I have, and I enjoy them. They remind us how soon a piano gets into a log hut on the frontier. Mr. Harte once sat at this very table when he came east on a reading tour. Lidian and I found him an easy, kindly, charming man, like his characters."

The train whistle sounds again.

"Lidian and I were conductors of the Underground Railroad."

The fugitive negro standing before me nods. I cannot guess his meaning.

"The Alcotts hid a runaway in their oven. The slave was small, and the oven wasn't lit."

What is it that you want, Emerson? Are you still curious, even now that you are drifting into the eternal backwater where salamanders have lost their fire and all that is left of the former music of the world is the plaints of peevish frogs?

I want to know whether to have been a slave is

the defining condition of a life or, in time, becomes an irrelevance.

Then ask him, Emerson, before your brain spoils, like a walnut turned rancid in its shell.

"Mr. Stokes, were you once a slave?"

"I suppose you want to hear my story."

"You're more than your story, James, but only by hearing it can I hope to know you."

"Is it important for you to know me?"

"If for no other reason than to satisfy my curiosity about another human being." Is it discretion, fear of his rebuff, or dread of his answer that prevents me from asking what I most want to know? Were you marked for life, body and soul?

I fill his glass. The ale seethes, as if the stars in the firmament were boiling.

"I belonged to Francis Parker, of New Madrid, Missouri. Along with his five sons, he farmed tobacco on the Mississippi at Kentucky Bend. He wasn't rich, as slaveholders go. He owned only six negroes, two of them women. I was seventeen and took care of the horses. He wasn't cruel by plantation standards; I recall that he whipped me only once, though it did take the bark off my back. But he held the papers on me, and, for that, I hated him."

Stokes raises his glass to drink, then sets it down, untasted.

"In the spring of '61, two of Parker's sons joined the Missouri State Guard, formed by Governor

Claiborne Jackson to stop the Union army from taking all of Missouri after St. Louis had fallen. Parker sent me along to do for them. We met up with Major General Price's men at Wilson's Creek, where the Guard, the Arkansas militia, and Confederate regulars had overrun the Federal boys and killed the Union commander of the Army of the West."

The evident pride he takes in his masters' rout of his liberators is another example of the cussedness of humankind.

"Full of beans, we beat the Yankees at the Battle of the Hemp Bales, named for the wet bales we wheeled ahead of us to quench the hot rifle shot as we went against the Union garrison. Mr. Emerson, we were chopping in high cotton! For a while, anyway."

He drinks some of the ale to make a space for his words to shape his recollection of those distant days.

"At the end of September, General John Frémont marched thirty-eight thousand Yankee soldiers a hundred and sixty miles west from St. Louis. At Sedalia, they backed us up against the Missouri River. The Parker brothers died inside a barn where we were hiding. I surrendered, and because I knew horses, I stayed with the Union cavalry. When the war was over, I was made a corporal. I would be still if I hadn't been in El Paso three weeks ago."

He subsides, of a sudden, like a hydrogen balloon when the gas leaks.

"Mr. Stokes . . ." No, no, I can't bring myself to

ask if slavery has altered his nub and essence, as it did his flesh. What would the lash have made of a boy's mind, so vulnerable and tender? I say instead, "You've done a good many things in your life."

"I wonder how many more I'll get to do."

We are both of us in the hands of the Presiding Judge, who shows no mercy.

"Mr. Stokes, do you have a wife?"

"No, sir."

"I've had two, have one still, whom you met."

The first, Ellen, gave me a youthful happiness, which comes to us but once. It lasted a year and a half, following an arduous wooing—the fault of my indecisiveness. Lidian, to whom I proposed without romance, in a letter delivered by the Plymouth postman, has been my long-suffering wife for forty-four years. (She does not seem ever to have been a bride.) She lives in a chamber of my heart next door to Ellen; they have never met and, therefore, never bicker. A superannuated god resides in the third chamber; the fourth is to let.

"And four children, one of whom died in childhood." Wallie, poor mite.

"I have a child by a Mexican woman."

Anticipating disapproval, Stokes glares. Because I spoke yesterday to Margaret Fuller, who bore a son without the blessings of the clergy, Roman or otherwise, I can return his defiant look with a beatific expression. That it is often seen on the faces of senile old men is beside the point.

"Does the child live with its mother?"

"With his Mexican grandmother in Parritas. His mother died last year of yellow fever."

Always death is the pivot on which a story turns. Even in geologic time, species, forms—the mountains themselves—must cease to be. And all the books ever written—even the one we call the Good Book—are pulp for wolfish time to fatten on. Not even God can escape the trap of time, because He made it with all-powerful hands. Nothing can undo the work of Omnipotence. And thus must God die, together with His creation.

"And you, Mr. Emerson, tell me yours."

"My story? It would take too long, not because I've done much that is remarkable but because I'm old, and my history would be as tiresome to relate as it would be for you to hear. But in payment for yours, I'll tell you mine, although very much abridged."

I'll keep to myself the revelation of the Artificer I received while standing amid the giant sequoias with John Muir. It was a moment of *tormenta* of the mind one would no more wish to share than the recollection of a first kiss.

Nor shall I tell Stokes of the moment in the Jardin des Plantes when I first perceived the upheaving principle of life. In the Paris botanical garden, I saw the manifold forms of creation arranged according to the taxonomy of the botanist Jussieu. I apprehended the web of analogy in which all matter is caught. In an instant, I traded the theology of the divines and the God of my fathers for the science of J. F. W. Herschel, who had written that systems of classification "have for their very aim to interweave all objects in a close and compact web of mutual relations and dependence." A thirty-year-old widower disenchanted by corpse-cold Unitarianism, I found myself moved by strange sympathies. The scorpions in the Cabinet of Natural History and the leopard in the menagerie were kin to me. My eyes were opened to a radiant truth as surely as Saul's had been on the road to Damascus, or Goethe's in the public garden at Palermo when he glimpsed *die Urpflanze,* the archetype of plants. Henceforth, my thoughts were not of God, but of nature—a force subsuming all other deities.

The memory of that brilliant afternoon nearly a half century past is not so bright now as a new penny. But beneath the tarnish laid down by time, the metal is unimpaired; indeed, its value has been increased a thousandfold by the dazzle of new things that have taken their place among the old.

Of daughter Ellen's and my five-week sail on the Nile aboard a dahabeah, I shan't say a word, either. The pyramids at Giza are cosmic reverberations of a principle whose meaning is lost to us, who respond only to a silence palpable as glass. Walking in their shadows, I was as exalted as Napoléon had been when he stood at night apart from his Grande Armée, like one in receipt of communiqués from the pharaohs.

One of my earliest memories of Father, the reserved and uninterested Unitarian minister—that, too, I'll keep to myself like a piece of chocolate set aside until one is in bed and should not be eating sweets. He took me onto a roof in Boston. I don't recall whether it was atop our house in Chauncy Street, First Church, or some other height. We watched the *Chesapeake* sail forth to do battle with the British frigate *Shannon* in Boston Harbor. Too soon our patriotic cheers turned to moans as the *Chesapeake* was boarded by the enemy's marines and taken as a prize. During the hand-to-hand combat, the American captain was mortally wounded. My father's death did not strike a greater blow to me than that brave man's.

I shall tell Stokes about my first encounter with Ellen Tucker, the girl I would marry and lose in almost the same breath. So it seemed to the grief-stricken husband who, even now, feels the pain of her loss like an amputated limb. The encounter was rapturous, like that in the Jardin des Plantes, which disclosed the occult correspondences by which nature is composed. Unlike it, the moment was constituted of a commonplace emotion that, nevertheless, exalts each individual in a fiery coronation. I tumbled head-long into love, which eludes Jussieu's system, existing, like the rose, to delight us.

"I met my first wife in that other Concord—the one in New Hampshire—where I'd gone to preach the Christmas-morning sermon. I was twenty-four; Ellen was sixteen. Two years later, in September 1829, we married. In February 1831, she died of consumption, in Boston, where I'd taken her to live after being called to minister at Second Church. Her passage was an agony. Neither God nor His son did so much for her pain as the opiates prescribed by Dr. Tarbell."

As a seamstress would, I bite the thread of my days and nights, leaving all the unsaid words like pins in my mouth.

"Mr. Stokes, I can say no more."

Stokes responds with a look that manages to convey sympathy, pity, and disappointment—the latter, likely, for the insignificance of the event he would assume to be my life's summit, as well as for the brevity of the tale. My life would seem puny to one who has gone deep into the marrow. I chose to live as a contemplative devoted to unraveling nature's mysteries to find the common thread. The homely one with which Lidian mends my shirts is also worthy of my regard, as is the seamstress herself, with her darning egg. Oh, but the realization comes too late!

Stokes's gaze settles on the oilcloth gashed from cutting pie dough into strips. If he is chewing on my words or letting his thoughts wander under less gloomy skies, I couldn't say—not even if I had all the words in Noah Webster's book at my tongue's service.

At birth, we are given shining rails to follow and allotted a portion of the right-of-way, which may be stony or fertile, according to the dogma of Calvinist election, a particle of grit in the works of the cosmos, a providential accountant's state of digestion, or Adolph Quetelet's statistics. The time must come when the wheels leave the tracks forever. Rust is our end, and a weedy lot our destination. "Deep in the man sits fast his fate." When I wrote that bit of pith, I believed that I was its master, that I bit my thumb at it. Now that my mortal form has begun to dissolve, I can more readily believe that man is the master of nothing, except the mummery of his life. We are hardly better off than old nags whose afterlife is the glue pot.

In Egypt, my daughter Ellen and I lunched with the Roosevelts of New York. I can see the hectic blue eyes of Teddy, the asthmatic boy with the dazzling teeth who ferried Nelly and me across the river at Assuan, below the first cataract. He and his father had been shooting birds and proudly showed me a peewit, a ziczac, two snipes, and eleven pigeons. I started to say that I would enjoy them more were they animate amid the papyrus and date palms growing along the ancient banks where ibises strutted than seen in a canvas bag, but Ellen bid me hush. I preferred Thebes, where I rode the English consul's Arabian around the ruined Necropolis. There I felt free.

Will we ever be rid of the hobbles of fate and

statistical predisposition and be able to ride the horse that now throws us?

Stokes coughs, as if to remind me of his presence. Sir, I have not forgotten you. I expect I'll remember you when all recollection of my earthly attachments is erased.

"I grow thin, Mr. Stokes. Soon the universe inside me will slip out like a yolk from an eggshell. Not even Ralph Waldo Emerson will ever put Humpty Dumpty together again."

With Lidian in mind, I tidy the sofa, where I spent an agitated night, and straighten one of Martin Heade's luminous storms of paint I knocked askew in its gilded frame. I glance out the window onto the pike, expecting to see Louisa May coming through the gate to collect her cloak.

I go upstairs to set to rights the room where Stokes spent his night. Made by the soldier in him, the bed seems never to have been disturbed by any mortal sleeper. Impulsively, I undress it of its Whig Rose quilt and sheet, get in, and, pull the bedclothes over me.

Emerson, what in God's name are you doing? What would Stokes say if he saw you? What would Lidian? What would Dr. Cowles, who supervises the McLean Asylum for the Insane? For what shall it profit a man if he shall lose his wits?

I want to breathe the air trapped inside the bed-clothes, in search of the odor of a negro. I want to mingle his atoms with mine. I may have left the church because I refused to believe that bread and wine can represent the body and blood of Christ— that wheat and grapes (even my neighbor Bull's Concord variety) can be alchemized into a man, for such I declare Jesus to have been, a man and only that. At this instant, however, I'd be willing to renounce Copernicus, who exiled humankind to the rim of the universe, and restore earth to its center, as Ptolemy had it, if only I could be changed. I wish to be imbued with the spiritus of James Stokes, permeating this bed even though I detect nothing but a faint odor of moth flakes. I want to burn in his naphtha—in the holy light by which Shadrach, Meshach, and Abednego danced.

What arrogance! What folly! But I breathe in, hoping to be transformed by another's atoms, though I know we are all one stuff.

"You're no better than a slaver, Emerson! You want to absorb a black man's essence and annex him to your own peculiar destiny."

"Brown, that isn't true!"

I'm defeated; I am laid low. I wish this bed were the last one of my mortal years, so that, having lain down, I would never get up from it again. I am tired of being in the world. I'm tired of being. The air is stale; it's been used up. There's not enough oxygen left to burn a candle. I wouldn't be surprised if the world outside the house were obliterated. Light or darkness, which of the two would be ubiquitous and evermore? I look out the window, into the yard. In the late-morning light, erect and uncowed, Mr. Stokes stands before Sam Staples, who, doubtless, has come to arrest the fugitive.

"Poor Jeoffry! Poor Jeoffry! The rat has bit thy throat."

Small bones snap underneath my stocking feet. All that remains of a peewit, a ziczac, two snipes, and eleven pigeons.

At the small bedside desk, I begin a letter to the president:

Dear President Hayes—

I draw your attention to the arrest of James Stokes, a corporal of the U.S. Army, Ninth Cavalry, Company L, under the command of Captain John Bacon, at Fort Bliss. Yesterday I gave Mr. Stokes sanctuary in my house, a humane service that I was happy to perform, because I am convinced, sir, that Mr. Stokes is a decent, honorable man.

The charge of murder that will likely be brought against him may be warranted in accordance with the laws of the state of Texas and the United States Army; however, his crime was the result of a provocation beyond the power of any

man to endure. I commend Mr. Stokes
to you and to your clemency.

Shall I be like Brutus on the Ides of March,
kneeling, bootlessly, on the Senate steps to beg Cae-
sar to forgive Publius Cimber? Are vain pleadings all
that can be done to save Stokes and the millions of
others yoked and bruised beneath some tyrant's heel?

> Emerson was a man
> Who walked round and round;
> And he wore a long coat
> That came down to the ground.
> Funny old man.

Old man, go practice your ice harp. Soon, soon
the threnody will sound, and you had better play it
well.

🌲

While dawdling at the top of the stairs, I smell
goulash.

Kossuth! I haven't tasted that peppery dish since
the Hungarian revolutionary stopped in Concord
during his triumphal tour of America. The town's only
Magyar made it in his honor for a party at Wright's
Tavern, on Lexington Road. Henry, Ellery Channing, Bronson, Sam Ward, young Frank Sanborn,
and I trooped noisily into the taproom, sat on hard
democratic benches, ate Mrs. Illényi's spicy dish (all

except Thoreau, who ate no flesh), and drank bumpers of lager beer to the exiled patriot Lajos Kossuth.

"Na zdrowie!"

Later, the tavern swelled with a deputation of Bostonians, who arrived on the Fitchburg train to ogle the man of the hour. He was a national sensation, feted at the Executive Mansion, invited to address Congress, and paraded on Broadway in a show of esteem rivaled only by that given to Lafayette and Buffalo Bill. The Bostonians among us wore enormous Kossuth cravats. They carried Kossuth umbrellas and clenched Kossuth pipes between their teeth. Dominions, kingdoms, and republics may fall to despots, as they will according to the savage processes of history, but enterprising men will find a means to enrich themselves even in a democracy. A resourceful Yankee will make money on a funeral.

"Na zdrowie, Lajos!"

We saluted him who declared that "the House of Habsburg-Lorraine, perjured in the sight of God and man, had forfeited the Hungarian throne" and who summoned the people to cast off the heavy yoke of the Austro-Hungarian Empire.

Following the Declaration of Hungarian Independence, proclaimed in May 1849, Kossuth served as governor-president of the Kingdom of Hungary until that August, when the imperial army of Czar Nicholas I crushed the Hungarian army and handed the nation to Franz Joseph I, emperor of Austria and now the apostolic king of Hungary, as well as secular king of Dalmatia, Bohemia, Croatia, Slavonia, Galicia, Jerusalem, et cetera. In 1852, I toasted Kossuth as "the foremost soldier of freedom in this age." In October 1879, he has come again to Concord.

"Lajos, are you really here, or do I mistake the tang of stale water in the vase where the chrysanthemums have wilted for the odor of goulash?"

"I haven't been near a bowl of paprika stew. But I'm here nonetheless."

He is standing at the end of the hallway. He resembles Alfred Tennyson in his old age, although the Hungarian appears dignified and self-assured in his, instead of merely bilious.

"You're very much changed, Lajos."

"I was fifty-one when I last visited Concord. We were nearly the same age then, and so must we be now, though the fire appears to have all but gone out in you, old man."

Against my will, my fists clench.

"Have you come to rebuke me for my wavering?"

"I've come to give you a swift kick in the ass."

I grip the banister, lest the fellow intends to actuate his violent metaphor.

"I suppose you are of John Brown's opinion."

"Természetesen. Naturally."

He relaxes his tone of voice and posture, and I my grip on the railing.

"I wish I could speak Hungarian, Lajos. It's strong and spicy, like goulash."

"You're speaking it."

I find this surprising because I have no fluency in any of the Finno-Ugric languages.

"You needn't have come, Lajos; I've decided to decide. I may do the bidding of fate and materialism, but I needn't be entirely at their mercy. I can choose to be free of their influence, if not wholly, then to the degree that my limited freedom and imperfect knowledge allow."

The remark pleases me and appears to satisfy him.

"Then I'll say búcsú.*"*

"Good–bye, Lajos. Long live!"

I glance over his broad shoulder into the room at the head of the stairs, hoping for a glimpse of Henry. In life, it was his bedchamber when he served in loco parentis during my absences from Bush. Just when I'd like a word with him, he's nowhere to be seen.

Starting downstairs, Lajos stops to ask whether Wright's Tavern still stands.

"It was on Lexington Road when last I looked."

"I won't ask you to join me, Emerson."

"No, I have urgent business here."

🌲

In the dooryard of my house, I take aim at Sam Staples. The rifle is uncommonly light. I do not tremble, nor does my heart play false. I sense no hesitation. My pulse registers no alarm. My heart lies easy in my chest. The time for meditation is past. Ralph Waldo Emerson is about to act!

How fine it is to renounce mind's sovereignty at last and to prick the bubble that encloses the rarefied atmosphere of a scholar who does not realize that he is slowly dying of asphyxia! How I delighted in the odor of old books, mistaking their must for frankincense! I watched the world go about its business from my writing desk. I looked at my ink-stained hands as though they bore the mark of a virtuous life. I looked at Lidian's hands after she had blackened the stove. Did she detect my distaste for menial occupations, which Henry undertook with gusto, as the psalmist David had done when tending his father's sheep before he was made king of Israel?

Dear Lydia, you threw yourself into the breach of abolitionism and woman's rights long before I came out for them. How proud I was of you on that Independence Day when, indignant, you draped black cloth over the fence in mourning for the slaves! After I shoot Sam Staples, I'll take Stokes north to Canada. I'll deliver him from his enemies and spend the balance of my days in the wilderness, a fugitive from the murderous American century. I'll grow my hair and beard like John Brown's and, like Henry, go huckleberrying. Now that my brain is becoming as an apple left to wither, I will live after the fashion of animals, whose thoughts are of earth and who raise their heads to the sky, though not in prayer. I've rid my eyes of the stye that blinds our kind to the truth.

Still, I am afraid.

Aunt Mary Moody Emerson's prescription rises from memory's compost and midden: "Always do what you are afraid to do."

Sam Staples turns to me. His face is kind. Does he see the fear in mine?

"Mr. Emerson, put down the broom. You've done enough."

John Brown leans against the elm tree, unknotting the noose that dispatched him in a field at Charles Town, Virginia, twenty years ago. He has worn it like a necktie ever since he accosted me at the fairgrounds.

"By God, he hasn't done enough by half! He has saved none, nor has he died for any."

"I'm not the Christ, John."

Henry and Hawthorne are playing mumblety-peg with Henry's old jackknife.

"He hasn't spent a single night in jail. Nathaniel, what do you say?"

As usual, the taciturn romancer has nothing to say.

"Waldo, you've been splendid!"

"Thank you, Margaret. You were always my friend. Any news from Fire Island?"

"Alas, no."

"Waldo, put down the broom."

Stokes buttons his blue serge coat.

"Mr. Emerson, I'm grateful, but I think I'll go along with the constable."

"Over his dead body!"

"John Brown, what is it that you expect from my old friend?"

"His martyrdom, Mr. Thoreau, nothing less than his martyrdom will do."

Henry throws his jackknife; it sticks in the elm beside Brown's head. Brown sniggers. I admired the zealot when he was alive; now that he's dead, I find him unpleasant.

Sam snuffles.

"Pshaw, Mr. Brown! I saw enough martyrs when I was in Rome."

"Miss Fuller—"

"Mrs. Ossoli, if you please!"

"Your courage has already been proved."

Sam produces a white handkerchief. I wonder, briefly, if he means to surrender, until he blows his nose in it.

"Why don't we go inside, Waldo, and talk things over?"

"I've been talking for three-quarters of a century and have little to show for all the noise and waste of breath."

"Now you know that isn't true, Waldo! You're the Sage of Concord, our town's greatest living man. You were a friend of Charles Dickens, Hawthorne, and who knows how many other famous folks. You were the best friend of Henry Thoreau, whom I had the honor of locking up for the night."

"The honor was all mine, Sam. I never slept so soundly as I did in your jailhouse."

Jeoffry trots across the yard. Held daintily between his teeth is a mouse, which he drops at Henry's feet, thereby affirming the uncanny gifts of the species *Felis catus.* The mouse runs for its life behind the rain barrel, attesting, by its exultant squeaks, to the truth of Christopher Smart's observation concerning *his* cat Jeoffry—*videlicet,* "one mouse in seven escapes by his dallying." My Jeoffry sniffs John Brown's boot with a "mixture of gravity and waggery." He visits Sam Staples next and scratches his trouser leg, as he would do a post to sharpen his nails. I think Jeoffry is a familiar sent me by Providence, "For he counteracts the powers of darkness by his electrical skin and glaring eyes." I sign myself like a Catholic, whose rites and customs are no more worthy of disdain than those of an ice-cold Unitarian or a disciple of Abner Doubleday.

Sam swats the cat, which camels his back, then trots away, his tail defiantly raised.

"Damn it all, Mr. Emerson, be reasonable! This man is wanted for murder, and I have to take him in."

"It isn't enough just to say the word *pear.* You must sink your teeth in it."

"It's all right, Mr. Emerson. I'll go with the constable."

"Mr. Stokes, I can't let you do that."

I round on Staples. "God is in this man. Would you take Him to your jailhouse?"

"Yes, if Judge Keyes gave me a warrant for His arrest. Stokes, it's time we were going."

"Waldo, dear, let the constable do his job."

"Is that you, Ellen? You know how weak my eyes are."

"It is, husband. You've been making quite a fuss. I could hear you in the next world."

"My brain's unwell, Ellen. I feel the seams of my skull opening like a rusty old boiler's."

Time has settled on me a dumb palsy—my portion of the fate that I've always sought to deny.

Ellen laughs, and I am made to think of roses and silver.

"Your ghosts are peeking out like a priest's cassock from underneath his alb."

"Or a Dutch gal's petticoat from beneath her skirts."

"Don't be coarse, Waldo."

"Ellen, it's been such a long time since I last saw you."

"Not since 1832, when you walked to Roxbury to visit my grave. My remains had not yet been removed to Mount Auburn, which is a much more pleasant place to lie. I thank you for it. But to open the coffin and look at me was unseemly, husband!"

"You saw me?"

"I was embarrassed by the smell and the state of my clothes."

She appears no worse for nearly a half century in the tomb.

"I had to prove to myself that you were dead. Something so very young and lovely—how could it be? I would have been a poor husband not to have given Hades a chance to change his mind and send you back to me."

"The jangle of your ice harp would not have charmed his savage breast!"

"I missed you so very much, wife."

"You've been a poor husband to Lydia."

The reproach is deserved, and well I know it, recalling that I once told Margaret Fuller that the universe was my bride. I made my wife—the second one, I mean—suffer by my folly. Vain posturing is laughable, contemptible even, never more so than in an elderly philosopher. But in spite of Ellen's chastening, I seem bent on perpetuating the image of the fatuous lover.

"The fire that captivated me remains even after all these years."

What mawkishness, Emerson, how like a mooning schoolboy!

"After all this time, mine has gone quite out, Waldo."

How wounding!

"The morning air is raw. Won't you let me rekindle the old flame that soldered us?"

She bridles indignantly. *"I beg your pardon?"*

"Don't misunderstand, Ellen; a conflagration, except for one I might produce in a heap of dead leaves, is beyond my waning powers."

"What fiddle-faddle! I do believe your wits have turned like poor old Bulkeley's."

I'm desperate to have her stay awhile. *"The grave's a cold and lonely place, my dear."*

"As if the soul requires mufflers, mittens, or Mrs. Winslow's Soothing Syrup!"

"As long as you walk abroad today, why not have a cup of tea and a digestive biscuit?"

She stares down her nose at me, as one might do a toad squatting in the path.

"Won't you at least say whether or not I was right to scorn the idea of a heaven?"

"Farewell, Waldo. Oh, the gift of white oak leaves you left on my coffin . . . It was a meaningless symbol, like so many others in your repertory."

Without another word, she leaves life's little stage for what is said to be reality, located on the other side of the proscenium arch. The golden trumpets of the morning announce her exit.

Sam Staples takes an ancient revolver from its holster. I doubt it's been fired since the War of the Rebellion.

"I'm too old to stand in the yard and jaw, Waldo.

Either we go inside and talk peaceably or I'm going to have to arrest you, too."

"Stick out your neck, Emerson. It's an old scrawny one, but it may be found acceptable to God nonetheless."

"John Brown, why don't you find some live coals to squat on?"

"What do you say, Waldo? Are you going to behave yourself?"

"Don't talk to my husband as if he were a child, Sam Staples!"

"Lydia! Is it you?"

"Who else? I took an early train."

She opens the gate and walks into the yard, carrying her satchel.

"I see you fixed the gate, Mr. Emerson."

"Yes, I did, Queenie."

"It squeaks."

"I'll oil it after I've seen to this business."

Sam returns the revolver to its holster. "I meant no disrespect, Mrs. Emerson, but your husband is interfering with the performance of my duty."

"Mr. Emerson, that's my best corn broom! For heaven's sakes, put it down!"

I see that I've been foolishly aiming a Shaker broom at Sam Staples. I surrender it to the constable, who gives it to Lydia, who leans it against the back door—but not before giving the doorstep a decisive domestic sweep.

"Why don't you come inside, Sam, and I'll fix you breakfast. You, too, Mr. Stokes."

"Thank you, ma'am."

Sam scratches his ear, weighing a temporary stay of justice against a good breakfast.

"I suppose it would be all right. I didn't get a chance to eat before Lyman Bierce came banging on my door."

I hiss. "The damned polecat."

"Are you hungry, Mr. Stokes?"

"I am, ma'am; thank you kindly." A soldier's appetite is truly prodigious.

"Come into the kitchen, you two. And wipe your feet."

Sam and James Stokes apply their boot soles to the scraper and troop into the kitchen.

"Kindly slice a loaf of bread, Mr. Stokes. Do you take your eggs scrambled?"

"That'd be fine, Mrs. Emerson."

I dawdle in the dooryard, not knowing what to do with myself.

"When I was in Florida, I ate alligator steak and boiled owl with a nephew of Bonaparte."

Since none appears to have heard my remark, I may not have spoken it aloud.

"Poke up the fire, Sam."

"Right you are, Mrs. Emerson."

"Coming, Mr. Emerson?"

"In a moment, Lydia." The gall, to have called her by any other name!

Louisa Alcott walks across the road. I expect she has come for her cloak. But it is the recent commotion that has brought the author of "blood and thunder" tales to my front gate.

"Waldo, whatever are you doing?"

"Did Bronson pull up the tracks in the cellar? It may not be too late to save James Stokes. Tell me, Lu, that the Underground Railroad still runs underneath Orchard House!"

She looks at me as though I were Nancy Barron crooning a mad song.

Standing in the dooryard, I bid farewell to "Old" Brown, who gives an equivocal nod of his head, which may be approbation or disparagement. His stern ghost flies back to his body, which lies a-mouldering in the grave. Go, blindworm, go.

I glance at the hemlock trees I planted when little Waldo was born, unless these standing tall before me supplanted them after they had fallen to blight, borers, or old age. We depart this world; that much is certain. We leave behind a measure of words according to our facility. If they be praised or belittled or even misunderstood is no concern of ours. More than likely, our eulogies will be fulsome, and the reports of our ill deeds inflamed.

In my fancy, I see Abe Lincoln on the steps of the bandstand. My fire out at last, I lie on the ground before him, together with all my dead. Using words spoken by the prince of Verona over the bodies of Romeo and Juliet, he declares, "Some shall be pardon'd, and some punishéd."

Will I taste sweet mercy or bitter inclemency? Or may it be, as I sometimes think, that the trump to awaken us to hear our doom pronounced will never sound at all?

L'envoi

*I*N THE SPRING, THE GOLDEN BEES of Pindus will
return to the garden, although I may not be here
to greet them. It little matters if I am not, so long as
some others are. I say, let all who will, pluck apples
from the trees and feast on pears, sacred to Pomona.
Let the gates of the poorhouse and the asylum be
unlocked. Let mad Nancy Barron out to play on the
banks of the river, amid willows, alders, and aspens.
Let God make good on the promises of His prophets.
We do not ask for manna, only for our daily bread. Let
the sacred books be kissed one last time before being
put away in the narrow cupboards of the spiteful. Let
places of worship be turned into schoolhouses. From
the winsome minarets let men and women be called
to study mercy. Let the roofs of the temples, mosques,
and churches be breached to admit the light and air
of the natural world, from which all truths radiate,
so that our children and theirs can greet the golden
bees in the one true paradise of the world before the
inward fire is quenched.

AFTERWORD

*T*HIS BOOK, THE TENTH IN The American Novels
series, reprises the principal themes that emerged
during their writing: the injustices that continue to vex
and vitiate the republic, the deaf ear many turn to its
tolling bell, our final estate and the meaning and purpose of our brief earthly tenure, and the use of language to discover and dissemble. Time and again, I
have written myself into a corner, pursuing an answer
to the old conundrum: whether individuals are obli-
gated to act against wrongdoing or are obliged by
uncertainty to "hang fire," in that picturesque Jamesian
image. Stated another way, the dilemma is this: If we
reject universal moral laws as an aspect of absolutism
and adopt relativism in their stead, how are we to judge
others and ourselves? The issue is not original, but it is
critical nonetheless. I am not excused from having to
confront it because I am unequipped to be a philosopher or a theologian or because so many other men and
women have struggled with it. Each of us is required to
take up the grave matters of the age and of the day, as
though no one before us has considered them.

In the present novel, Ralph Waldo Emerson,
toward the end of his life, is obliged, by the arrival of

a black deserter, to make an ethical choice. Naturally, I can only imagine how Emerson the idealist and stoic would have acted or failed to act. I am the author of his crisis, as well as of its resolution; his choice—the one I give him—therefore may have more to do with me than him, of the me I wish myself to be. (Resolutions occur more often in literature than in life.)

To speak publicly against slavery in the violent years leading up to the Civil War took courage, even in New England. Emerson did not become active in the abolitionist movement until August 1844, seven years after his wife Lidian had done. In the fiction I have set in 1879, he faces, in the concentrated form of drama, the moral dilemma that he faced prior to the Civil War, in which the dilemma *seemed* to have been resolved. (More than a million men, north and south, were gored on its horns, to use the old metaphor.) It continues to divide us. (The January 6 insurrection and its aftermath show us how much.)

Emerson's responsibility to the just treatment and well-being of all men and women did not end with a proclamation or a constitutional amendment, nor did ours. So must we also choose to act—not once, at a crucial moment in our personal histories, but as many times as we are confronted by injustice or abuse. As Lincoln said in his second inaugural address, "with firmness in the right, as God gives us to see the right, let us strive on to finish the work we are in . . ." (Emerson came to believe utterly in

Lincoln, although he would not always believe in or love God, or any other deity, save that which men and women contain within themselves, where heaven is.) The work *we* are in is not yet finished. And I have not always shown the courage of my convictions.

My aim was to write neither a biography of Emerson nor a historical novel; nonetheless, I tried to be as true to his character and to that of the historical personages surrounding him as I was able. Liberties were taken in the interest of storytelling. For example, Orchard House, where the Alcotts were living at the time this novel is set, is not so near to the Emersons' on Cambridge Turnpike as I have made it seem. I have made Lidian, who was a chronic invalid, more energetic than she was at this time in her life. I hope not to have misrepresented the ideas of actual people, and I beg the pardon of students and scholars for my errors.

Emerson's writings, life, and the necessary business of his life were extraordinarily various, as perhaps only those of a nineteenth-century personality could be. In his adage "A foolish consistency is the hobgoblin of little minds," he seems to license inconsistency (never mind the qualifier "foolish"). In fact, he is referring to the developing consciousness, which constantly corrects itself in accord with changing information and experience. Emerson's view on many subjects, such as science, community, abolitionism,* and the purpose of life, changed over time. In my portrait of him, the way stations of his thought appear not in the order of their arrival but as they would to one whose recollection is as unreliable as an obsolete timetable.

Postscript. I applied the final coat of polish to this novel during the third week of Russia's war against Ukraine. Like most others of the world, I am compelled to watch this most terrible of current events. I tell myself that it is the duty of every human to bear witness. But is that enough? John Brown would say no. A year from now, when this book is read, if there is a world left in which to read it, I may have my answer.

---

* As late as August 1852, Emerson wrote of his failure to throw himself into "this deplorable question of Slavery," maintaining that "I have quite other slaves to free than those negroes, to wit, imprisoned spirits, imprisoned thoughts, far back in the brain of man,— far retired in the heaven of invention, &, which, important to the republic of Man, have no watchman, or lover, or defender, but I."

Acknowledgments

"The greatest genius will never be worth much if he pretends to draw exclusively on his own resources." Goethe wrote that, and Emerson quoted him, and years later, Robert D. Richardson, Jr., quoted Emerson quoting Goethe. For this book of mine, I have drawn from Richardson's quotations from Emerson's writings, as well as from primary sources. I was well served by his *Emerson: The Mind on Fire*, as well as by Carlos Baker's *Emerson Among the Eccentrics: A Group Portrait*. Both books were essential to shaping my view, however flawed and imperfect, of the brilliant, restless mind of the Concord genius—Richardson's for his study of Emerson's consciousness and the thought that informed it, and Baker's for his portraits of the Transcendentalists and other literary personalities in Emerson's orbit. Without those two books, much of the meat of my story would have been off the bone. As I write this, I am aware that Emerson would have frowned on my experiencing him through anyone else's work but his own.

The title *The Ice Harp* was suggested by his journal entry on December 10, 1836.

Of additional assistance to me were the American Transcendentalism website; the online *Stanford Encyclopedia of Philosophy*; *The Oxford Book of Children's Verse*, edited by Iona and Peter Opie; *Walt Whitman Speaks*, edited by Brenda Wineapple; and the King James Bible (1769 Oxford edition). For Emerson, the Bible was not a book of ancient prophecies and revelations, but a work of moral philosophy valued for its ethical precepts, a text he considered neither more nor less divinely inspired than the dialogues of Plato, the Upanishads, *The Four Books* of Confucianism, or the *Meditations* of Marcus Aurelius.

I thank Coleman Barks for allowing me to excerpt from "Gnats Inside the Wind," his translation of *Mathnawi* III: 4624–59 ("Some gnats come from the grass to speak with Solomon" and "gnat plaintiffs") by the thirteenth-century Sufi mystic poet Rumi, whose work Emerson admired.

I have sometimes put into the mouths of the principal characters their actual spoken or written utterances, without acknowledging them by quotation marks. I believe the marks would have distracted and, perhaps, confused readers, who, I hope, will set disbelief aside and consider my amalgam of monologues, soliloquies, and conversations genuine. (Literary scholars will separate the nuggets from my fool's gold.)

Once again, I am indebted to Bellevue Literary Press, especially to its publisher and editorial director,

Erika Goldman, without whose persisting faith this book and likely the entire series of American Novels would not have gone abroad, doing, it is to be hoped, some good in the world. In an age when the loudest voices seem to shape the national discourse, quiet, reasoned, but no less impassioned, utterances need to be heard. Admirers of truth and beauty—I embrace both—should give thanks to presses committed to the difficult business of their dissemination.

BELLEVUE LITERARY PRESS is devoted to publishing
literary fiction and nonfiction at the intersection of
the arts and sciences because we believe that science and
the humanities are natural companions for understanding
the human experience. We feature exceptional literature
that explores the nature of consciousness, embodiment,
and the underpinnings of the social contract. With
each book we publish, our goal is to foster a rich,
interdisciplinary dialogue that will forge new tools for
thinking and engaging with the world.

To support our press and its mission, and for our full
catalogue of published titles, please visit us at blpress.org.

BELLEVUE LITERARY PRESS
New York